MIND GAP

MIND GAP

Marina Cohen

DUNDURN PRESS
TORONTO

Project Editor: Michael Carroll
Copy Editor: Cheryl Hawley
Design: Jesse Hooper
Printer: Webcom

Library and Archives Canada Cataloguing in Publication

Cohen, Marina
    Mind gap / by Marina Cohen.

Issued also in an electronic format.
ISBN 978-1-55488-801-6

    I. Title.

PS8605.O378M56 2011   jC813'.6   C2010-902445-1

1   2   3   4   5   15   14   13   12   11

We acknowledge the support of the **Canada Council for the Arts** and the **Ontario Arts Council** for our publishing program. We also acknowledge the financial support of the **Government of Canada** through the **Canada Book Fund** and **Livres Canada Books**, and the **Government of Ontario** through the **Ontario Book Publishers Tax Credit** program, and the **Ontario Media Development Corporation**.

Printed and bound in Canada.
www.dundurn.com

Dundurn Press	Gazelle Book Services Limited	Dundurn Press
3 Church Street, Suite 500	White Cross Mills	2250 Military Road
Toronto, Ontario, Canada	High Town, Lancaster, England	Tonawanda, NY
M5E 1M2	LA1 4XS	U.S.A. 14150

For Martha

ACKNOWLEDGEMENTS

I would like to send a heartfelt thank-you to the following people: to readers, Dr. David Jenkinson, Mac Martin, Nora Tuchagues, Dave Benner, and 7B; to Phil Perlmutter for assisting me with legal terminology and Kevin Klayman for sharing his "street" knowledge; to my husband, Michael Cohen, for his love and support; to my agent, Margaret Hart; and to the amazing staff at Dundurn Press, including president and publisher Kirk Howard, associate publisher and editorial director Michael Carroll, and my editor, Cheryl Hawley.

CHAPTER ONE

"In or out?"

Jake shaded his cards with his left hand. He peeled up the corners with his right. Two of clubs. Ace of spades. He glanced at the cafeteria table. Face up, in a neat row, lay the seven of diamonds, the two of hearts, and the jack of clubs. *Deuces,* he thought. *Story of my life.*

"Come on, man — in or out?"

Over the hum of gossip, the shuffling of feet, and the grinding of chairs, Jake heard a twinge in Cole's voice. He looked up, and their eyes locked for a second. Jake could read his best friend like a cheap magazine. Cole had a big mouth, but he got nervous quickly. He was bluffing.

"In," said Jake, tossing his second dollar into the pile. He shifted his gaze to the dealer.

Damon was more difficult to read. From his greasy hair to the tattoo of a crown dripping blood emblazoned across his knuckles, all the way down to his brand-new Nikes, the guy was stone cold.

Damon threw a buck into the pile. He kept his grey eyes trained on Jake as he slowly flipped over another card and placed it next to the jack. Queen of clubs.

Cole checked and began chewing his lip.

Too obvious, thought Jake, battling the urge to smile. He pushed a stack of four quarters into the growing mound. Jake had a lousy hand, but at this point he had nothing left to lose.

Damon answered.

Cole shook his head and swore. He threw down his cards and began shovelling fries into his mouth. Cole seemed to take his losses much harder these days.

Damon flipped over the final card, dragging Jake's attention back to the game — ace of diamonds.

Two pair, thought Jake, *ace high. Nice.*

Jake willed his pulse to slow. His mouth was a thin line. He ran a hand through his thick hair. Then he picked up his last stack of coins and tossed them casually into the heap. Nine bucks. Ten, if Damon continued. Not what you'd call a fortune, but hey, it was better than a poke in the eye with a sharp stick. Jake slipped his hand into the pocket of his jeans. He shifted his cellphone. Stray nickels and dimes danced between his fingers. If he lost this hand, he could kiss next week's lunches goodbye. Like he'd done this week. And last.

"Call," said Damon. He placed his two

cards onto the pile of money as though he were claiming it. He had a pair of aces.

Jake let out his breath. The deuces came in handy, after all. He turned his cards over one by one. Jake watched Damon's eyes darken. Suddenly, they reminded Jake of shark eyes — cold and lifeless. Jake stretched out his arms to rake in his winnings.

"Why, gentlemen," said a deep voice, "you wouldn't happen to be partaking in the quite illegal and most suspendable act of gambling, would you?"

Jake peered over his shoulder at the towering six-foot-six figure of his English teacher, Mr. Dean.

"At the very least it would mean a week's worth of detentions for each of you."

Cole could wriggle his way out of a clogged pipe. Trouble was, his mouth was quicker than his brain. "Gambling? *Us*? Course not, sir. We're just having an enjoyable game of Fish. And this money here?" He jerked his chin toward the pile. "Why, it just happens to be sitting on the table doing nothing." He sat back looking pretty proud of himself.

"Nothing?" Mr. Dean frowned. "Hmm, I see." He scratched his chin, then volleyed glances from Damon to Cole, finally settling on Jake. "Well, if this money is just doing *nothing*, then I'm sure you gentlemen wouldn't mind if I donate it to the Salvation Army where it can do *something*?"

Jake rolled his eyes and scowled, but kept his mouth shut.

Mr. Dean patted Jake on the shoulder. "Life is an endless series of choices, Mr. MacRae." He leaned in, scooped up the loot, and strolled off, humming "Amazing Grace."

Jake gave Cole a shove. "You idiot."

"What'd I do?"

"This money just happens to be sitting here doing nothing ..." Jake mocked. "Couldn't you have come up with something better?"

"I didn't hear anything brilliant shooting out of your mouth. And I guess you'd have wanted a pile of detentions instead?"

Jake picked up his cards and threw them across the table.

Cole sneered. "Think of it as bail."

Damon was leaning back in his chair. "Forget it. It's chump change. Let's talk real business."

Business. Right. Jake had avoided thinking about it all day. He reached over and grabbed a few fries from Cole's plate. They were cold and tasted like cardboard.

"My brother says you guys have been hanging around the coffee shop long enough. He wants you to do a favour for him."

Damon's brother, Vlad, was what you'd call *king* of the 5 King Tribe. He was the kind of guy you did not want to disappoint.

"We're in," said Cole all too eagerly. He glanced at Jake, but Jake didn't say a word.

"Good," said Damon. "Vlad will be happy."

"So, um, what exactly does he want us to do?" asked Jake.

Damon was eyeing him as if they were playing poker again. Only this time Jake felt his cheeks flush.

"Meet at the coffee shop at one o'clock on Sunday. Pick up a package and take it to where Vlad tells you. A simple delivery."

Simple, thought Jake. *But what if simple gets complicated?*

"Delivery," said Cole. "Sure." He flashed Jake another look. This one said: *Be cool.*

The bell rang, ending second lunch. Damon grabbed the cards, shoved them into his pocket, and swaggered off into the stream of students heading toward their lockers. "Sunday," he called over his shoulder. He didn't look back.

"What's your problem?" asked Cole once Damon had disappeared. "Don't you get it? When Vlad asks you to do something, you do it."

Jake didn't respond. His thoughts were doing backflips.

"It's just a delivery," said Cole. "Like Damon said — simple."

"Simple," echoed Jake. He was nodding, but his expression betrayed his uncertainty.

Cole sighed. "Make up your mind, man — in or out ...?"

CHAPTER TWO

The October sky looked like an art experiment gone wrong. Blotches of red, orange, and purple streaked the deepening blue as the sun hovered low in the horizon. It was getting dark earlier. A bitter wind raced down the street, scattering litter and leaves. It sliced through Jake's grey hoodie, chilling him to the bone. He bent his head and hugged his chest. He was late and he hadn't called. His mom was going to go off like a firecracker.

Jake slipped inside the building. While he waited for the elevator, he thought up excuses.

Team tryouts? Nah. She'd never buy it.

Detention? Sure. But then he'd catch it just the same.

Extra help? Jake smiled — even *he* wouldn't believe that.

The elevator doors opened, and Jake stepped inside. He pressed number seven and felt the old motor kick in as the traction steel ropes began hauling him upward. Then somewhere between the third and fifth floors the elevator ground to a halt and the lights went out. In the ten years he'd lived in the building this had never happened.

Jake stood for a moment, searching the darkness. It was thick and complete. The tiny space seemed to be drawing in on him, getting hotter by the second and leaking oxygen. Jake's pulse quickened. Sweat skittered across his forehead. He reached out, fumbling for the emergency button. Then a voice — more like a whisper of wind — blew past his right ear.

Last stop.

Jake spun round. He stepped backward until he was against the metal doors. *Who had said that?* But before his brain could calculate possibilities the lights went on, the air cooled, and the elevator jolted upward. Jake was standing alone. His eyes swept the ceiling and floor. A wad of gum. A cigarette butt. A chocolate-bar wrapper. He mopped his forehead and took a deep breath, exhaling slowly. Must have been his imagination.

Exiting the elevator, Jake headed down the hallway. There was barely enough time to turn the key before the door to his apartment flew open.

"Where have you been? How many times do I have to tell you to call?"

The fireworks display began.

"Do you ever listen to a word I say? I feel like I'm banging my head against a wall."

Jake stood there, letting his mother finish her rant. There was no point in stopping her.

Once she got going, she'd have to say it all. If he interrupted, her lecture would never end. He'd learned that the hard way.

"Why didn't you answer your phone?"

"It was off."

"Perfect. Why do I bother paying for that thing?" She leaned in closer and sniffed. "Have you been drinking again?"

"Huh? No." Jake shrugged and did his best to look indignant. Like it had never happened before.

Jake's mother's stringy blond hair was showing an inch of dark roots. The corners of her eyes were ploughed like fields. She was skinny. Too skinny. She wore jeans that were out of style and T-shirts that were too big. She looked way older than thirty-four.

"I'll bet you were hanging around with *Cole*." She said his name as if it were some kind of disease. "I don't trust him. He's a cheap thug. He's been getting you into trouble ever since you met him."

Just then Drew poked his head round the corner. He mimicked their mother, shaking his head, gesturing, and moving his mouth exaggeratedly. It made Jake smile.

"Oh, I suppose you think I'm funny now. Some kinda joke. Well, let's see if you think it's funny when I …"

"No, Mom," said Drew, stepping into the hallway. "He's not laughing at you … it was me …"

"Save it, Drew. You're always trying to rescue your brother. But I got news for you — he isn't the one who needs rescuing …" She said this last bit to herself as if neither of them would understand it, anyway.

She turned back to Jake and whispered, "He thinks you're some great hero. He'd jump off a bridge if you asked him." She glared at Jake for a second longer, then her eyes softened and she reached out and hugged him. She pushed away and shook her head. With disappointment weighing her face, she grabbed her pack of cigarettes from the hall table and walked toward the balcony. "Dinner's in the kitchen. It's cold."

Jake dropped his backpack by the door, kicked off his shoes, and strolled into the living room. "Get out the Xbox. I'm gonna kick your butt in Karate Chaos." He plunked himself onto the sofa. Jake was still a bit edgy from the elevator experience and figured playing a game or two would calm his nerves. The Xbox was an old hand-me-down. He wished they had one of those new high-tech systems. If only his luck would change, then he'd be able to earn back some of his losses and buy one.

"You wanna piece 'a me?" said Drew, grinning. He got out the controllers and turned on the TV. "So how'd it go today? Did you win?"

The money. Jake cleared his throat. "Oh. Yeah. Yeah, I won, but ..."

"Cool! So where's my money?"

Jake took a deep breath. His brother's eyes were so wide and happy that Jake had to look away. "Well, thing is ... well, this teacher came and, well ... he kinda confiscated the cash." Jake glanced at his brother. The smile remained on his face, but the light in his eyes had dimmed.

"Confiscated?"

Jake paused. "He took it."

The corners of Drew's mouth quivered, but he kept on smiling.

CHAPTER THREE

Jake lay on his bed, his eyes closed, his iPod cranked to the max. Drew was watching his favourite reality show. Jake loved his time alone — and in the one-bedroom apartment there was never enough of it. Once nine o'clock rolled around, Drew would come bouncing into the bedroom, and Jake would no longer have the space to himself. He'd have to listen to his ten-year-old brother yak on and on until Drew finally passed out. Jake glanced at his alarm clock. Fifteen more minutes of peace.

As bass bludgeoned his ears, Jake thought about the 5 King Tribe. How cool would it be to be a real member? Guys to watch his back. Security. Belonging. Respect. Power. But there was other stuff, too. Stuff that worried Jake.

His phone vibrated. He dug into the pocket of his jeans and pulled it out. It was Cole. Jake shut off his iPod. "What do you want?"

"Nice greeting."

"I'm bagged, man. What's up?"

"Flash party."

Jake sat up. The rusty bed frame creaked. "Party? Where?"

"No idea."

Cole was one of those guys who dragged everything out, like a cat playing with a mouse before he ate it.

"That's stupid. How can you not know where?"

"It's a flash party. Could be anywhere. At a house. In an alley. In a barn …"

Jake sighed. "Okay. So how does it work?"

"You'll get a text later tonight. It'll tell everyone where to meet. You won't know where until the last minute. What do you think? You in?"

In. Out. In. Out. Jake's thoughts were spinning again. "I dunno."

"Come on," Cole whined. He paused, then pulled out his ace in the hole. "Shelly might be there."

"Shelly? You sure?"

"I can't guarantee she'll show, but she'll get the text."

Jake stood up. He walked over to the bedroom door and opened it a crack. His mother was sitting beside Drew on the sofa. "What time?"

"Late," Cole said. "So?"

Jake watched his mom put her arm around his little brother. Drew was the perfect son. He did well in school. Never got into trouble. Jake and his brother were like night and day. Jake couldn't seem to stay out of trouble. His mother would skin him alive if he snuck out again. She caught him once and nearly kicked him out. She gave him the silent treatment for an entire week. Wouldn't say a single word to him, as if he didn't exist.

"I dunno …"

Cole sighed dramatically. "Jake … Jake … this is so you. You say you wanna be cool. You say you wanna hook up with Shelly. Then you get a chance and you chicken out. You're such a loser."

Cole's words stung. "Watch your mouth."

"Whatever," said Cole. "You'll get the text. It's up to you."

Jake stared at his phone for a second, then pressed end.

Another decision. Why couldn't life be simple? No problems. No decisions. Jake suddenly wished he was a wild animal. A wolf. A *lone wolf*, sitting pretty at the top of the food chain, with nothing and no one to worry about. Except maybe his next meal. Or the odd hunter. Or a possible run-in with an angry bear. And then there was the deterioration of his natural habitat …

Okay, so life sucks even for wolves, he thought.

Anyway, he'd made up his mind. Shelly or

no Shelly, he was tired. He wasn't going to any stupid flash party.

Just as Jake lay down again, his bedroom door burst open. His mother stood there with that crazed look she got when Jake had done something really horrible.

"I can't believe you!" she hissed.

Jake winced. This wasn't good. For a second he wondered if she'd overheard his conversation with Cole. Maybe she had his room bugged.

"I can't believe you did such a rotten thing!"

Did? That was the past tense. Jake took a deep breath. Whatever it was, he'd already done it and she knew about it. No use in trying to talk his way out.

"Where's Drew?" he asked.

"Brushing his teeth." His mother eyed him with disgust. "How could you take your little brother's money and gamble it away?"

Jake rolled his eyes. The money thing again.

"It's bad enough you gamble your own money, my money, money I work hard for and give to you so you can buy lunch and clothes, but now you have to gamble Drew's money away, too?"

"Listen, Mom ..." he tried.

"Don't *listen Mom* me! I've had enough of you. Lazy. Irresponsible. You're throwing your life away, you know that? You're so selfish. You're exactly like —"

Jake sat up and cut her off before she could finish. "Like who? The Pigeon? Is that who I'm like?" He glared at her.

She closed her eyes. When she opened them again, her expression had changed. She slumped against the wall as if her bones had evaporated. Then she took a deep breath and exhaled. "I didn't say that."

"But you were thinking it," he snapped.

Whenever his mother compared him to his father — the father who had abandoned them when Drew was a baby and Jake was only four — Jake went ballistic. He barely had any memory of the guy, yet he hated him. He didn't refer to him as Dad or even by his first name. He called him "The Pigeon" because, as his mom always said, "He flew the coop."

"Listen to me, Jake," she said. "You can be anything you want to be. You just gotta make the right choices."

Jake hated it even more when she got all philosophical on him. She sounded exactly like Mr. Dean. And what did either of them know, anyway? Truth was, he couldn't be anything. Not like Drew. Not like the smart one, the good one. If Jake wanted respect, he'd have to take it. Steal it. Like Damon and Vlad. Like the 5 Kings ...

"Do I look like him?" he blurted out "Is that it? Is that why you hate me so much?"

He stared at her, waiting for something, anything, to tell him he was wrong. Seconds felt like hours. He gritted his teeth and flung himself back onto his bed, turning to face the wall.

"I *love* you, Jake …" Her voice trailed off. He could feel her stare pulling at him, trying to turn him around. He imagined the sticky-sweet smile masking her real feelings.

"Please, Jake," she tried again. "I'm just tired. I can't hold your hand anymore. You're not a little kid. You're going to do what you want to do. But it's killing me. I feel like I'm just standing there watching you throw it all away."

Her words hung in the air like a rotten odour. She was giving up on him. He could feel it. Maybe she already had. Maybe she drove his father away by nagging him all the time, too. Maybe it was all her fault.

Just then Drew bounced into the room. "You're not going to believe who they eliminated!"

His mother sighed and left the room. Tears burned at the back of Jake's eyes, but he held them prisoner. Drew went on and on about the show until he finally wore himself out.

For the longest time Jake lay awake thinking about his father. Why did he leave? Where did he go? His mother never talked about him. She'd thrown away all his pictures. Jake couldn't even remember what he looked like. He was a phantom haunting the hollow rooms of Jake's mind.

The only clear memory Jake had was of the time his father bought him a shiny red toboggan. It was mid-October and wouldn't snow for quite a while, but his dad had promised that the very first snowfall they would go tobogganing together. By the time the snow arrived, his father was long gone. Jake kept that toboggan for years. Then one day he walked to the curb, tossed it onto the trash, and stood watching as the garbage truck crushed it.

Jake took a deep breath and closed his eyes.

He was four years old, riding down the perfect hill covered in December snow. Strong arms cradled him from behind, helping him steer. He could feel icy wind on his cheeks, hot breath on his neck. Deep laughter filled the air. He was happy.

Then the landscape began to change. The white snow turned city-slush grey. The arms steadying him disappeared, and the laughter faded. Jake was alone, and the toboggan was out of control, flying faster and faster, heading straight into darkness. Something was in that darkness, and he was headed straight for it. He was going to crash. Jake lifted his hands to shield his eyes. He opened his mouth to scream. He sat bolt upright in his bed.

His cellphone was buzzing.

CHAPTER FOUR

St. George Station. Southbound train. Midnight.

Jake stared at the text and yawned. He rubbed his eyes. A party on a subway. At midnight. He had to admit he was curious.

He glanced at his alarm clock. It was 11:07. Jake did some quick calculations. If he even wanted to make it to St. George Station by midnight, he'd have to hurry. It was a twenty-minute bus ride from his building to the subway. From there he'd have to catch a westbound train, ride thirteen stops, and then switch to the north-south route. It would be tight.

Jake could hear his brother's heavy breathing. Drew wouldn't be a problem. Jake could set off a bomb and his brother wouldn't so much as stir.

His mother was another story. She slept on the pullout sofa in the living room and was known to wake up if a cockroach scuttled across the floor. The last thing Jake wanted was to be caught. He reconsidered, almost climbing back into bed, but then his mother's face flashed before him and he remembered that awful look in her eyes — the look that said she'd given up on him — and it was as if someone had dumped a bucket of ice water over his head.

A party is exactly what I need, he thought. *She already thinks I'm like The Pigeon — so why disappoint her?*

Jake groped around the floor for his jeans. He pulled them on and shoved his cellphone and iPod into his pocket. Next he grabbed his black hoodie — it was clean and lay folded on top of his dresser. Just in case Shelly did turn up, at least he'd smell good.

Slipping out of the bedroom, Jake crept toward the front door. For a second he thought he'd heard the sofa groan. He held his breath, but the apartment was still. Jake moved swiftly, stepping into his running shoes and clicking the deadbolt. If he swung the door open quickly, it wouldn't creak.

The hall lights were dim. They masked the cracks in the walls, making the building seem almost livable. The stench of other people's cooking saturated the air — cabbage, fish, and a clash of spices that made Jake's stomach turn. He raced along the worn carpet toward the elevator, but when he reached it he did an about-face. Jake told himself the stairs would be quicker, though deep down he knew he was still spooked by the freaky incident.

Stale smoke and urine battled for control of the stairwell. Jake hurried down flight after flight until he reached the main floor. He pushed open the door and stepped out into the cool of the night.

It must have rained. The air was heavy and the sidewalk was slick. Jake turned on his iPod as he flew down the empty side street toward the bus shelter. More than once he got the feeling he was being followed, but quick glances over his shoulder confirmed he was alone.

Even this late, buses ran frequently along the main routes. Jake stood in the shelter and watched cars zip past, bass pulsing through his body. He checked his phone for the time. It was already 11:15. If the bus didn't come soon, he might as well turn around and go home.

As he waited, his thoughts drifted back to his father. Had the guy snuck out in the middle of the night? Had he jumped on a bus and never looked back? What could possibly make someone abandon his family?

A blast of toxic air scattered Jake's thoughts as the bus shrieked to a halt in front of him. He hadn't even seen it coming.

Jake climbed aboard, paid his fare, and grabbed a transfer slip. As the vehicle lurched forward, he swaggered to the back where he plunked himself into the last row. There were several other passengers on the bus, none of whom paid Jake any attention. He leaned his head against the window, took a deep breath, and shut his eyes.

Last stop.

Jake's eyes snapped open. His pulse thrummed. *Who had said that?* Jake searched his surroundings. There was no one even close to him. He must have dozed off, because the bus was already pulling into the subway station. Was he imagining things again? *Last stop?* Those words wormed their way around and around in his head.

Jake checked his cell. It was 11:37. There was no time to waste. He flew up the aisle, jumped off the bus, and headed down the steps into the station.

During the day, Victoria Park Station was a hive of activity. Although far from empty, Jake could hear the thud of his footsteps echoing through the hollow hall as he made his way toward the ticket booth. He tossed his transfer to the attendant, pushed through the turnstile, and broke into a sprint as the familiar thunder of an approaching subway shook the ceiling and walls. Jake made it to the platform just as the westbound train exploded into the station.

The subway car was pretty full. Jake slumped into a seat and cranked up the volume on his iPod. He leaned back and was about to close his eyes again but reconsidered. This time he'd keep them wide open.

He scanned the car. There were two kinds of people in the subway this time of night. Either they had that listless quality about them — as if they were heading home from late-hour jobs — or they were buzzing with electricity — as if they were heading out for a big night on the town.

A group of teenagers were goofing around at the opposite end. Jake wondered if they were going to the same party. One girl was looking directly at him. He didn't want to be caught staring, so he shifted his gaze to the advertisements lining the tops of the windows. His eyes settled on one sign in particular. It read: KILL THE LIGHTS. SAVE THE BIRDS. It had a picture of a black-headed bird with a white breast flying over brightly lit office buildings at night.

The advertisement made Jake think of pigeons — flying the coop.

CHAPTER FIVE

Station after station, people entered and exited the subway, each oblivious to the other's existence. Jake decided he could spend his entire life riding aimlessly, never seeing the same person twice.

He checked his phone: 11:55. One more stop — plenty of time.

The group of teenagers had left the train. *Too bad*, thought Jake, *that girl was pretty hot.* As the subway began to roll, Jake settled back and relaxed. He was confident he'd make it to the party on time. He had more than four minutes and this was a short stop. Then, just after the train entered the tunnel, it ground to a sudden halt.

Figures, thought Jake, ripping off his iPod and shoving it into his pocket. *Can't anything ever go right?*

Seconds passed like hours. He kept checking his phone. Three minutes left. Two minutes …

The subway finally lurched forward and started picking up speed. It slithered through the dark tunnel like a snake into its hole. When it burst through the darkness and into the station,

Jake had one minute left. He was already standing at the doors waiting for them to open.

Luckily, there were few people to get in his way. He sprinted the length of the platform until he reached the escalator. The ceiling above him began to quake. He took the steps two at a time, but halfway up stood a man in an old trench coat muttering to himself. The man took up the entire space, blocking Jake's path. He smelled like egg salad left too long in the sun.

"'Scuse me," Jake said, but the guy didn't budge.

The thundering had stopped. Jake needed to get around this guy and quick. With a twinge of disgust, he used his shoulder to muscle past the man, nearly knocking him over. The subway was straight ahead — its doors open wide. Jake raced toward them, then heard the familiar chimes announcing their closure. In a last-ditch effort he lunged to try to stick his hand between the doors. He missed by an inch and nearly got his foot stuck in the gap between the subway and the platform. The rubber panels sealed themselves tight. He was too late.

All Jake could do was stand there and watch helplessly as the subway rolled into motion. Car after car glided past him, leaving nothing but stale air blowing through his hair. When the train had disappeared into the tunnel, Jake's eyes settled on the red triangular warning sign posted on a black pillar between the tracks. It had a stick man crossing from the platform onto a train. It said: MIND THE GAP. Beside that was a large poster in the centre of the tracks. It was an ad for the latest teeth whitener. Five people of various ages and ethnicity stared at him with ridiculous grins. It was as if they were all mocking him. *You're a loser, Jake, just like Cole said.*

"The bowels of hell await you!"

Jake swung around to see the guy who had blocked his way on the escalator staggering toward him, pointing a dirty, accusing finger. The ends of his coat were frayed. His shoes were mismatched. His beard was long and dishevelled. He looked — and more importantly *smelled* — as if he hadn't bathed in years. Unmistakably homeless. There was no telling how old he was. Could be thirty. Could be fifty. Street life wasn't easy on the complexion.

"Judgment is upon you!"

Perfect, thought Jake, rolling his eyes. *Exactly what I need.*

"Lay your hands in mine!"

Grease and dirt were caked on the guy's face, but Jake noticed a strange spark in his eyes. He held both hands outstretched as though he were coming to hug Jake.

"Rise up from the darkness! Take my hands and rise!"

Rise. Riiiight. Nutjob. Jake rolled his eyes. He was about to head back toward the escalator when he heard a low rumble. Instinctively, he glanced up. The clock on the flat-screen monitor still read twelve o'clock. He walked to the edge of the platform and peered into the tunnel. There was a dim yellow light getting brighter by the second.

"They're coming ... take my hand ..." the man muttered.

A train was approaching at top speed, its headlights unusually bright — so bright Jake had to shade his eyes. It blasted into the station, rushing past him, its roar drowning out the lunatic raving behind him. But as Jake's eyes adjusted to what he saw, he frowned. Instead of the modern steel-grey subway, what blew past him was an old maroon train with two thin gold stripes. He recognized it from a news story he'd once seen about the transit system. It appeared to be one of the original subway trains — the Gloucester.

I thought they'd retired those dinosaurs decades ago, thought Jake as it screeched to a halt and the doors opened. But as quickly as they opened, they began closing again. Without a second to think, Jake stepped inside. The last thing he heard before the doors sealed themselves was the homeless man's voice echoing through the hollow station: "You have entered the belly of the beast …"

The lights dimmed, then brightened, then dimmed again. The car rattled and shook as it lurched forward. As he scanned the interior of the car, Jake grabbed for the nearest pole to steady himself.

If this was a party, it was the weirdest one he'd ever seen.

CHAPTER SIX

The inside of the train was dim. It smelled like a pile of dirty laundry. Passengers were crammed like cattle. Some were laughing. Others were talking. Music — the kind you might hear in the bathroom of a fancy hotel — wafted above the crowd.

One guy was wearing a grey sweatshirt with cut-off sleeves and matching sweatpants. Over his sweats he wore red shorts — short-shorts, like the kind basketball players wore in the 1980s. He had sweatbands on his wrists. Another guy had greased-up hair and a retro leather jacket like some James Dean wannabe. A neon-green mohawk sprouted from one girl's head. She posed in skin-tight leopard-print pants and the pointiest boots Jake had ever seen. Another girl wore a dress and shoes that must have belonged to her great-grandmother. Still another looked like a hippie, complete with fringed vest and headband.

A costume party, thought Jake. It was Halloween in a couple of weeks, and it figured that Cole would leave out the most important detail.

Jake scanned the crowd, looking for his buddy, but as far as he could tell Cole had stood him up. As he looked around, he noticed some of the passengers staring at him and whispering to one another.

"I'm going to kill you, Cole," he muttered under his breath.

"You can't kill anyone," said the guy in the short-shorts. "We've already tried that. It's been done to death. Literally." People around the guy burst out laughing as if he'd just told the funniest joke in the world.

"Um, yeah," said Jake. "Whatever."

Something really weird was going on. Jake could feel it in his gut. Hopefully, the train would get to the next station quickly so he could jump off and make his way back home.

"So. You wanna party ...?" asked Short-Shorts. His dark eyes narrowed. "Have you, uh, got a ticket?"

"Ticket?" Jake mumbled. Instinctively, he dug in his pocket and produced the wrinkled transfer slip. The train got suddenly quiet. He could feel eyes crawling all over him. Everyone was staring at him except one girl who sat facing the dark window. She was holding a little pink blanket in her arms and rocking back and forth. There was another passenger who wasn't staring at him, either. A guy sitting all alone. Before Jake could catch a glimpse of his face, ice-cold hands swung him around.

"Just passing through, eh? One of the lucky ones. Better hang on to that transfer. You never know when it might come in handy."

Jake wondered if these people had escaped from an insane asylum. The homeless dude on the platform should have gotten on the train instead. He would have fitted right in.

"I think I made a mistake," said Jake.

"Maybe," said Short-Shorts. "Then again, maybe not ..." He grinned as if he'd said something really funny again.

"I don't want any trouble," said Jake. "I'm just going to get off at the next stop." He turned to face the doors. This stop was taking forever. The old pot lights kept flickering. The subway car rattled as it curved through the tunnel. Was it Jake's imagination or was it getting warmer?

"Get off at the next stop?" Short-Shorts shook his head. "You're pretty funny, you know that?"

Jake could see the guy's refection in the dark glass of the subway car doors. His face was distorted, his grin maniacal.

Come on, subway. Next stop should be coming right up ...

Jake felt a hand on his shoulder.

"I said, you're one of the lucky ones."

"Get lost, man," Jake said, spinning around. He shoved the guy, sending him careening into a group of passengers. They caught him and burst out laughing.

Short-Shorts steadied himself and began moving toward Jake again. Jake braced himself.

Just then the subway ploughed into the station and slowed. Jake didn't want to turn his back until the last second. Finally, the train came to a complete stop, and he heard the doors open. Jake turned to exit, but when his eyes settled on the black writing on the walls of the station, the air caught in his lungs.

He stepped off the train and back onto the very same platform he'd left from.

As the doors behind him closed, a voice like sandpaper scraped at his ears: "You can get off, Jake ... but you can't leave ..."

CHAPTER SEVEN

Jake felt as if he'd just stepped out of a nightmare. His head was a cyclone of thoughts. He moved back until he felt himself up against the cold tile wall. Jake took a deep breath and let the air escape slowly as he watched the last car disappear into the tunnel.

The platform was empty, but it was St. George Station, all right. Jake stood motionless for a moment, letting the storm in his mind settle. He examined his surroundings. Something was different — something he couldn't quite put his finger on. Then it hit him. The plasma screens were gone. They were replaced with digital clocks that read exactly midnight. How was that possible? How could a subway leave a station and re-enter the exact same one at the exact same time? And who had taken the monitors? And how had that guy on the train known his name?

Jake ran a trembling hand through his hair. "I just need to get home and get some sleep," he muttered. The sound of his own voice was comforting.

As he walked toward the escalator, he dug into his pocket for his iPod. He froze. It wasn't there. Neither was his phone. Or his keys. Or his wallet. He searched frantically, checking each of his pockets and the floor, but it was no use — they were gone! They must have fallen out on the train during his scuffle with Short-Shorts. Either that or someone had stolen them. Even his transfer slip was gone.

Jake smacked his hand against the grimy wall and swore. "This night is getting better by the minute."

Resigning himself to the fact that his stuff was lost, he took the escalator to the lower level and headed toward the eastbound platform. Since he hadn't actually exited the transit system, he didn't have to pay another fare. This was a minor relief since all he had left were the stray nickels and dimes he hadn't gambled away — and even those had mysteriously dwindled in number. Jake hit the button on the transfer dispenser and shoved the new slip into his pocket without even glancing at it.

The train came quickly. A regular train — nothing old or odd about it. He boarded and sat back, thankful he was heading home.

Jake yawned deeply. He stared off into space, wondering why he had let Cole convince him to go to the party in the first place. To stay awake, Jake read the ads. There was an ad for some store's upcoming sale, but the clothing seemed out of style. There was a Microsoft ad for Windows that looked ancient. *How long has that been hanging around?* Jake thought. Then he saw the subway map. It showed the north-south route and the east-west route, but the new line was missing.

Suddenly, something else occurred to Jake. Back at St. George Station the ad for the teeth whitener was gone. He remembered staring at the smiling faces before he'd boarded the old train, but it hadn't been there when he'd gotten off. Where were the flat-screen monitors and where were the smiling people?

Questions flooded his mind again. No matter which way he looked at it, nothing made any sense. Was his memory playing tricks on him? Was he going crazy? Or had Short-Shorts slipped him something?

He shook his head. Impossible. He hadn't had anything to eat or drink. He checked his exposed skin. He'd once read you could be drugged using a Band-Aid-type patch, but there was nothing there — nothing that might explain all the weird stuff that was happening. Jake slumped back into his seat. He was exhausted. That must be it. What he really needed was sleep. Everything would be clearer in the morning.

Aside from a shift change in the attendant, Victoria Park Station looked pretty much the same as when he'd last seen it. Jake's bus was already waiting. He climbed onboard, flashed the new transfer slip to the driver, and shoved it back into his pocket. He sat down, leaned his head against the window, and watched the houses and buildings fly by. Jake knew a way to get into his building without his keys, but how would he get into his apartment without waking his mother?

CHAPTER EIGHT

Jake searched for lit windows and counted balconies. Someone was awake on the ninth floor of his building. He'd used this trick once before when he forgot his keys. Jake entered the foyer and buzzed the lit apartment.

"Yeah?" asked a voice.

Jake covered his mouth with his hand and mumbled something incomprehensible. The buzzer went off. Pulling open the door, Jake slipped inside.

He was so relieved to finally be home that even the old building looked somehow fresher. Cleaner. "Now," he said, stepping into the elevator, "if I can just survive the fireworks …"

Jake stood outside his apartment door, bracing himself for the worst his mother could unleash. He knocked quietly at first so as not to wake Drew, but when no one answered, he tried again with a bit more force. Ten seconds passed. Twenty. Still no one came.

That's weird, he thought. His mother was such a light sleeper he was sure she'd come flying. A sinking feeling returned to the pit of Jake's stomach. He clenched his fist, and this time he pounded on the wood as hard as he could. Shuffling and swearing came from inside the apartment and then heavy footsteps approached.

"Who is it?" demanded a crusty voice on the other side of the door. "Whaddya want?"

Jake's pulse quickened. Whoever that was, it wasn't his mother. He stepped back and checked the apartment number. It was his. He took a deep breath. Maybe he hadn't heard correctly. Maybe his mother had a cold or something. He cleared his throat. "It's me. Jake."

"*Jake?*" asked the voice. "Jake who? I don't know any Jake."

Was this some kind of warped joke? Could Drew be behind this?

"If that's you, Drew, you'd better let me in right now or I'm gonna —"

The deadbolt clicked and the door opened a crack. A sliver of unshaven face with a bloodshot eye peered through. The eye sized Jake up and down.

"Get lost, kid, or I'm gonna call the cops," the guy snarled. Then the door slammed shut, and Jake heard the man cursing as his footsteps retreated. "Stupid teenagers ... drunk ... waking people up ..."

It was as if someone had sucker-punched Jake, knocking the wind right out of him. It took a few seconds for his brain to convince his lungs to start breathing again.

Had his mother found out he'd snuck out? Was this her way of teaching him a lesson? For a second Jake thought about pounding on the door again and demanding to be let in, but something held him back. That guy — whoever he was — had been pretty convincing.

Jake was exhausted and confused. If his mother really wanted to punish him, he'd go along with it. He'd wait until morning and then try her again. He wandered to the end of the hallway, plunked himself down, leaned his head against the wall, and closed his eyes.

CHAPTER NINE

"Get up, kid. Let's go."

Jake felt a strong hand on his shoulder. He rubbed his eyes and opened them.

"Come on. You can't sleep here. Move it."

Jake looked up at a man's face — a familiar face — and he breathed a sigh of relief.

"Hey, Mr. Borrelli," he muttered. "Am I glad to see you."

The man took a step back and narrowed his eyes. "How do you know my name?"

Jake steadied his hand against the wall and stood up. His body ached. He felt as if he'd been asleep for centuries — like that fairy-tale character. What was his name? Rip Van Something. "Good one, Mr. B. You're too funny."

The man stared at Jake for the longest time, not saying a word. Then he grabbed Jake by the shoulder and pushed him toward the elevator. "I don't know who you are or how you know my name, but you can't stay here. Go home, kid, or I'll have to toss you out."

Jake planted his feet. He swung around and eyed the superintendent of the building with a mixture of anger and disbelief. There was something different about him. He had less grey hair and looked somehow ... younger.

"It's me, Mr. Borrelli. It's Jake in 710. Where's my mom, and who's that guy in our apartment?"

Mr. Borrelli leaned in and sniffed. Satisfied Jake was sober, he let go of his shoulder. "I have no idea who you are or where your mom is, kid. Mr. Banks lives in 710. You don't wanna mess with him. Come on, let's go. Or do I have to call the police?"

Jake fought hard to hold it together. He forced out his words to stop them from shaking. "Please. Just tell my mom I've been punished enough. I get it. I've learned my lesson. I won't sneak out again. Just tell her to let me back in, okay? Please?"

Mr. Borrelli guided Jake to the elevator and ushered him inside. As they descended, Jake continued to plead. "Come on, Mr. B. Just let me talk to my mom. I know she's mad now, but she's been mad before and it always blows over ..."

They reached the lobby. Mr. Borrelli pulled Jake toward the front door. Before he pushed him out he must have seen the helplessness in Jake's eyes, because he stopped. When he spoke again, his voice was kinder. "You okay, kid? You need a few bucks?"

Jake shrugged. He didn't know what else to say.

Mr. Borrelli reached into his pocket and handed Jake a five-dollar bill. "Go home, kid. Whatever it is, it can't be that bad." He let the door to the building slam shut.

Jake sucked in a lungful of early-morning air. He wrapped his arms around his chest and walked across the street to the coffee shop where he bought an orange juice and a bagel. He stared out the greasy window and watched the sun spill over the horizon, splashing the streets with gold. In another hour he could go to Cole's house. The way he saw it, Cole owed him. It was his fault Jake was in this mess. Jake would hang out at Cole's until his mom cooled off and decided to let him come back home.

Beside Jake sat a hefty, bearded man gulping a large coffee and inhaling a Danish. He was reading a newspaper, and when he got up, he left it lying on the table. Jake reached over and picked it up. He took a swig of coffee and a bite of his bagel and scanned the headlines: PLANKTON MAY PROTECT PLANET FROM ICY FATE … FURTHER STEPS TO ENHANCE U.S. MARITIME SECURITY … FREEZE ON GENETIC MODIFICATION ENDS IN NEW ZEALAND … BUSH ECONOMIC PLAN SUPPORTED …

Jake frowned. "*Bush?* He hasn't been president for …"

It hit him as suddenly and as hard as an anvil to his gut. He nearly choked on his bagel as his eyes zipped to the date at the top of the page.

"What the?" he gasped. But even as the words left him the shop began to spin. The whole world started to spin. The newspaper fluttered to the ground. Jake felt as if he were being flushed down a toilet. As his mind struggled to stay afloat in the whirling gush of thoughts, bits and pieces bubbled to the surface: The building looked newer. Mr. Borrelli looked younger. The ad for an old Microsoft Windows. His iPod and cellphone gone. The old transfer gone, too …

Jake shook his head. It was an old newspaper the guy was reading. That had to be it. He forced himself into motion. He reached into the pocket of his jeans and, one by one, pulled out the coins: a dime dated 1972, a nickel from 1985, two more dimes dating back to 1996, and a quarter from 2000. Nothing — not a one — older than that. With trembling hands he dug into his pocket again and produced the transfer he had taken from the machine a few short hours ago. He unfolded it. The date was printed in bold black letters. The world around Jake crumbled.

CHAPTER TEN

Jake's legs felt like jelly as he moved toward the counter. A woman was busy arranging a fresh batch of doughnuts with a pair of metal tongs. Everything was happening in slow motion. The sounds around him were muffled, movements blurred. He cleared his throat, and the woman turned to face him.

"Can I help you?" she asked.

"Uh ..." he began, not quite sure how to phrase his question. "Can you tell me what day this is?"

The woman's dreary expression morphed into a puzzled look. "Saturday," she said. Her gaze lingered on him, somehow sensing there was more.

Part of Jake didn't want to continue, but he had to know for sure. "And the date?"

She tucked a loose strand of dark hair behind her ear and folded her arms. No doubt wondering where this was heading, she raised her chin slightly. "The eighteenth."

Jake winced. He knew how ridiculous he was going to sound, but he had to proceed. "The ... *year*?"

The woman eyed Jake suspiciously as if he were a few cards shy of a full deck. Her voice dropped. Jake watched her lips moving, forming each and every number carefully, but it was as if he'd suddenly lost all hearing.

Jake closed his eyes. He could feel the blood draining from his face. It was true. It was real. Jake had somehow travelled ten years back in time!

He took a deep breath, trying to calm his nerves, then opened his eyes. He turned to leave, barely making it halfway to the door before his knees buckled and he slumped into a seat near the front window.

There was no point in going to Cole's house. Cole wasn't there. There was no point in going anywhere. No one would be home.

Jake sat in the coffee shop for the longest time, staring into space, trying to convince himself this wasn't happening. Cars zipped up and down the street. Even the shiny new ones looked somehow old to Jake. Maybe if he sat long enough he'd wake up from this nightmare. Maybe he could sit there for ten years.

"You can't stay here forever," said the woman as she approached Jake. "If you're not going to buy anything else, I think you'd better leave."

Jake must have spooked her, because she stayed at a cautious distance and kept glancing around at the other customers, perhaps wondering who'd come to her rescue if Jake went berserk. But Jake didn't have the energy even to argue. He stood up and exited the shop without saying a word. He was sure she kept watching him until he was out of sight.

As he wandered aimlessly down the chilly street, he tried to put the pieces together in his mind. No matter which way he looked at it, everything came back to that subway. It had happened there. Somehow that freaky old train had taken him back in time. But how? And why? And more important, how was he going to get back to the future?

Jake's mind was hazy. He wasn't paying attention to where he was going. The traffic light was still red when, without thinking, he stepped onto the road. A car swerved to avoid hitting him, and Jake fell backward, slamming onto the curb. The car screeched to a halt, and the driver sprang out.

"What are you doing?" the man shouted as he ran toward Jake. "Trying to get yourself killed?" He dragged Jake off the road and onto the sidewalk. "Are you okay? Should I call an ambulance?"

Jake's back was sore, but he managed to stand. "I'm fine."

The man narrowed his eyes. "You don't look okay." He paused, then suggested, "How about I drive you home?"

Home. Jake smiled bitterly. He had no home. He was homeless. Maybe he would end up like that crazy guy on the subway platform. He shook his head. "I'm okay."

The man pulled out a black thing the size of a small brick from his jacket pocket, and it took Jake a few seconds to recognize that it was a cellphone. "Come on. Let me at least call someone for you. Your parents maybe?"

It was as if a light had switched on in Jake's mind. The haze evaporated, and he suddenly knew exactly what he had to do. He scrambled to his feet and took off running.

"Thanks, man!" he called over his shoulder.

The driver yelled at Jake, "Hey, wait!"

Jake was furious with himself for not thinking of this right away. He knew exactly where he had to go. The only problem was — he wasn't sure how to get there.

CHAPTER ELEVEN

The woman behind the counter jumped as Jake burst back into the coffee shop. She brandished her metal tongs as he charged toward the counter. He was panting and his eyes were fierce.

"There isn't much money in the cashbox!" she yelled. "Just take it! Don't hurt me!"

Jake stopped short. His brow crinkled. "*Hurt* you?" He stared at her as if she had three heads. Then he glanced at the other customers who were sitting stock-still, watching him wide-eyed. Suddenly, it occurred to Jake what they must be thinking. He took a step back and waved his hands in front of his face. "You've got it wrong. All I want is a phone book."

The woman's fingers tightened their grip on the tongs. "A *phone book*?"

Jake nodded. "I need to borrow one. It's urgent. Have you got one?"

She paused for a second, gaping at Jake as if she couldn't quite decide if he was an idiot, a maniac, or a little of both. Without taking her eyes off him, she reached below the counter and hauled out an enormous book. It landed with a thud in front of Jake. When he reached for it, the woman took a step back.

Although the cover looked new, it already had numbers scrawled all over it and even a doodle in the shape of two hearts. Jake opened the book midway and flipped through chunks of pages at a time: *K*, *L*, *M* ... Ma, Mabley, MacArthur, Mackinnon ... MacRae.

Jake's heart plummeted six storeys. There must have been a hundred of them.

Out of the corner of his eye he saw the woman dialling the phone, but he was so focused on his task it didn't register.

"I've gotta find it," he muttered to himself. He gripped the page and tore it clean out. "Sorry," he said to the woman, but she was too busy talking on the phone to acknowledge him. Jake left the shop as quickly as he'd entered it.

Standing on the curb, he scanned the length of the page. It wouldn't be listed under his mother's name, and there certainly wouldn't be an entry for Pigeon MacRae. Jake wracked his brain. He'd heard his mother mention their previous address a few times. He remembered the street had a name that reminded Jake of fish. Trout Street? Tuna Lane? He searched the list, thinking so hard that he didn't even hear the sirens.

"Sammon Avenue!" he shouted. "That's it!"

The sirens were getting louder.

Pleased with himself, Jake took a deep breath and a good look around. The lady and the two customers were standing right up against the window of the shop, gawking at him. He almost gave them a friendly wave, but his brain jump-started, and it suddenly dawned on him — the sirens were approaching, police sirens. That lady had called the cops!

Up the street, Jake saw flashing lights. Whatever he decided to do, he had to do it quickly. He'd done absolutely nothing wrong, but what in the world would he say to the police if they questioned him? *Yo, dudes. Don't mind me. I'm just some guy from the future.* Best-case scenario: his butt would land in a mental health facility. Worst-case scenario … well, there was no time to contemplate that. He had no wallet. No ID. No home. No one to call. No matter which way he looked at it, there was only one choice he could make — *run!*

Shoving the paper into his pocket, Jake bolted behind the coffee shop and into an alley. He hopped a fence and raced through someone's backyard and onto a side street. Jake could hear the police sirens blaring. They must have reached the coffee shop. He flew down the street until it wound around back onto the main road.

Jake stopped running to attract less attention. Across the street a large grocery store welcomed customers. He ducked into it and took a deep breath once he reached the produce section where people calmly sifted through the various fruits and vegetables. Jake was pretty sure the police had better things to do than to conduct a full-blown manhunt for some crazy, confused teenager who'd stolen a page out of a phone book and freaked a few people out. Still, with everything that was going on, Jake couldn't be sure of anything anymore.

CHAPTER TWELVE

Jake stood across the street from the house. It looked nice. A nice little house. It had beige siding and brown shutters that gave it a cottage feel. A large pine tree loomed in the centre of the lawn, partially obstructing Jake's view of the front door. A vision flitted through Jake's memory. Warm sunshine rained down on him. He was collecting pinecones — his arms so full that for each pinecone he picked up, three slipped through his grasp. How old could he have been? Three? Four?

Two hours ago Jake had been so sure he wanted to see this place. He had asked everyone in the grocery store if they knew where Sammon Avenue was. No one knew. He asked a few people if they had a BlackBerry or an iPhone. They looked at him as if he were speaking a foreign language. Finally, a woman said she kept a map in the glove compartment of her car, and together they located the street. It was a quick jog down Victoria Park and then a long walk across O'Connor.

And now here he was at the exact place he wanted to be, and yet, for some reason it felt ...

wrong. Jake was alive ten years ago. He was four years old. What would happen if he came face to face with himself? He'd once read a book where someone changed something really minor in the past and that change rippled outward with horrible repercussions. What if coming face to face with himself created some sort of cosmic paradox vacuum and he and his four-year-old self ended up cancelling each other out of existence?

Jake's thoughts swarmed but then scattered when the front door of the house swung open. A figure appeared. It took Jake a moment to recognize his own mother. His pulse quickened. Until now everything had felt like a crazy dream — a nightmare — but for the first time it all became painfully real. Tears pooled in his eyes.

Even at a distance she looked so much younger. Her hair was styled, her face less drawn. Her movements were lighter — nothing weighed her down. His mother bent to pick up a newspaper that lay on the front step. She looked up, and her gaze settled on Jake. He wanted to charge toward her, throw his arms around her, and scream, "It's me, Mom! It's Jake!" But he bit his lip. Her eyes lingered on him a second longer, then she grasped the paper, stepped back into the house, and pulled the door shut.

A chilly gust of wind swept the street. Jake felt colder than he'd ever felt before. He shouldn't have come here. What had he hoped to gain? They wouldn't know him. He would be a stranger to them — a crazy stranger.

Jake turned to leave. He had only taken a few steps when, out of the corner of his eye, he saw the door open again. He turned around. This time a man stepped out of the house. He walked down the driveway toward the street. For a second Jake thought he was coming to confront him, but then the man turned sharply and headed in the opposite direction.

It was his father. Jake was sure of it.

Without thinking, Jake did an about-face and began trailing the man. Each step he took shuddered through his body like a warning. This was wrong. Really wrong. He shouldn't meddle with fate. Yet his desire to meet the man — the phantom — who had haunted his mind for ten long years was too intense to dismiss. Jake couldn't stop himself.

As he stalked his father, Jake started to calculate. The timing was right. Could it be? Could this be the day his father left home for good? He had no suitcase with him. No bags of any kind. Dressed in a regular pair of jeans and a regular jacket, there was no neon sign on him flashing: LOOK AT ME! I'M DUMPING MY FAMILY. Then it occurred to Jake. Maybe that was why it had hurt his mother so much. Maybe that was why she could never talk about it. Maybe there was nothing to say. No big fight. No grand finale. No bells ringing the curtain down. Maybe she never even saw it coming.

At the main road Jake's father headed south. Jake followed, staying close enough to keep him in sight, but far enough to remain unnoticed.

Time didn't pass — it melted. Slowly, steadily, like a Popsicle in the sun.

At an intersection Jake's father halted at a red light. Jake stopped at the curb right beside him. His heart in his throat, Jake stole a sideways glance. His father couldn't have been more than thirty, and he didn't resemble Jake at all. In fact, his father looked a lot like Drew. Part of Jake had hated the thought of resembling the guy who had abandoned him, but part of him clung to that idea, as if it was the one tie his father couldn't sever. Disappointment draped over Jake's face like a dirty dish towel.

Where was this man going? To work? To visit a friend? He could be going to buy ice cream for all Jake knew. Anger sloshed around the pit of Jake's stomach, churning to bile. He could just as easily be a pigeon flying the coop.

CHAPTER THIRTEEN

Jake had lost all sense of time and place when they walked into the subway station. Following his father mechanically, Jake lost sight of him once as he stopped at the ticket booth. Jake felt in his pocket. Luckily, he still had the change from the five bucks Mr. Borrelli had given him, but was it enough? Jake handed the attendant a handful of coins. The man frowned and then sifted through the pile until he'd counted a dollar forty. Fares were a lot cheaper ten years ago. Jake took a transfer and scrambled after his father.

A train came quickly, and Jake got on it without thinking. Time and space ceased to exist.

Jake plunked himself into a seat across from his father. He kept his eyes trained on him the entire time, scrutinizing the man's every move. Every scratch, every tilt of his head, every shift in position told a story Jake had been longing to hear.

Inside Jake's head a battle raged. *Should I talk to him? Should I say something? What should I say?*

Why do I even want to talk to him? I desperately want to talk to him and I hate myself for it.

Curiosity gave way to anger. Jake couldn't help but think about all the missed opportunities. They had never played basketball. They had never watched a hockey game. His father hadn't been there to help Jake with his homework or flip out at him about his low grades. He hadn't been there the time those older boys had stolen Jake's toque and pushed him into the snowbank. He hadn't been there to teach him how to ride a bike or throw a football or play poker or ...

Jake's father stood up and walked to the subway doors. Jake followed as though drawn by an invisible string. He stood right behind him, tasting his musky cologne. Jake wanted to grab the guy and spin him around. He wanted to shake him. To punch him. To hug him tightly and never let go.

The doors opened. His father stepped off the subway and strolled calmly toward the escalator. Consumed with conflicting emotions, Jake didn't even notice they had arrived at St. George Station. They rode the escalator up side by side, and suddenly Jake felt his father's eyes on him, staring at him as if noticing him for the very first time. Jake's heart tunnelled through his ribs. It was now or never. Should he say something? He'd be taking a huge risk. Just like in that weird sci-fi book he'd read, the effects could be devastating. Jake chewed his lip. It wasn't worth it. *He* wasn't worth it. Jake had to let it go. Let *him* go. Jake took a step upward when he felt a hand on his shoulder.

"Do I know you?"

Jake nearly lost his balance but grabbed the railing and steadied himself. He couldn't bring himself to look his father in the eye. He swallowed a boulder-sized lump in his throat. "N-no … I don't think so …" he stammered.

"Because you look really familiar," continued his father in an infuriatingly kind voice.

Jake shook his head, keeping his eyes to the ground. "You got the wrong guy …"

They had reached the top of the escalator. *Keep walking*, Jake told himself. *Walk away.* Jake moved through and around clusters of people toward the southbound platform, his father glued to his side watching him — the hunter now the hunted. Jake stepped toward the edge, standing right on the yellow warning strip.

The sign straight ahead read: MIND THE GAP.

"I'm sure we've met before," said his father. "I never forget a face."

Like the last drop of water that split the dam, Jake couldn't hold it together any longer.

All the things he'd ever wanted to say to his father, everything he'd kept bottled up inside him all those years, gushed out of him in waves of incomprehensible blather.

"I can't believe it's really you. You shouldn't have gone. I hated you for it. We all hate you …"

The smile faded from his father's lips.

"Why did you do it?" Jake continued. "Where did you go? How could you? How could you just up and leave like that … like you're doing right now? You're going, aren't you? You're not planning on going back home, right?"

Jake's father took a step backward. He looked at Jake the same way the lady in the coffee shop had. Jake moved closer to him, his accusations relentless.

"Do you have any idea what it did to Mom? I've never seen her happy. Not ever. You shredded her heart, you know that? Because of you she cries every night. Because of you …"

Jake's father stood on the yellow warning strip close to the edge, his expression clear — he thought Jake was unstable.

"Look, kid, I was wrong. I don't know you. I'm sorry …"

"Know me?" Jake moved closer to his father, who was backing up along the yellow strip. "Of course, you don't know me! You left before you got a chance to know me. I'm Jake! Your son!

I slipped through some kind of tunnel in time, and I'm here to tell you you suck, man! You suck big time!"

Jake's father's eyes were as wide as chasms. "How ... how do you know my son's name?"

"I know his name because I'm him! I know how crazy this sounds, but it's me, Dad, it's Jake! I'm fourteen freakin' years old, but it's me!"

A yellow light radiated from the tunnel, growing brighter by the second. The platform trembled. A train was approaching. Jake glanced around. None of the other people on the platform seemed to notice.

"You're crazy," said his father. "I don't know how you know my son's name, but I'm warning you —"

Jake laughed like a lunatic. "*You're* warning *me*? What a joke! Your threats mean nothing. Your words mean nothing!"

Thunder rumbled down the tracks. The light was so bright that Jake had to squint. He refused to let up, though. This was his one chance to say everything he'd ever wanted to say.

Jake's father turned his back. He started to walk away.

"Just like the red toboggan!" he shouted over the roar of the approaching subway. Tears streamed down his cheeks.

Jake's father froze.

"And just like the promise that came with it! You said we'd go out together on the very first snowfall. We never did. We never went because you dumped me. You dumped us all!"

Jake's father swung round to face him just as the old Gloucester came barrelling into the station. It was exactly twelve o'clock, and suddenly it became clear to Jake what was happening. The old train flew by, its rush of stale air pressing Jake's eyelids shut. When he opened them, the doors were ajar. The same weird people were crammed into the car, laughing and partying. No one else on the platform even appeared to see the train, let alone its passengers. Just Jake. It had come for him. This was his ride home. No matter how much he wanted to stay, he knew he had to get on.

Jake stepped inside the car, but just as the doors began to close he felt a hand grab his arm. He spun round. His father stood on the platform, staring at Jake wide-eyed, trying to pull him off the train. Everyone in the car started to laugh — a horrible sound like the noise a bunch of wounded animals might make.

"Let go!" Jake cried. But even as the words left his mouth, he saw the three-inch gap between the subway and the platform double, then triple its width. Jake's father clung tightly to him, as if he recognized Jake and wasn't going to let him go.

Something was wrong. Terribly wrong.

Jake shouldn't have talked to his father. He shouldn't have had any contact with him. The doors remained slightly ajar. Jake could see the gap between the platform and the train getting larger and larger. A great black hole opened up like the mouth of a mythical beast.

"Let go, Dad!" he screamed. But it was too late. His father had slipped off the platform and was dangling over the abyss. He clung to Jake, nearly yanking him off the train in the process. Jake grabbed his hand and pulled with all his strength, but his father was too heavy. He was slipping. Jake couldn't hold on much longer. Then, for one fleeting moment, it was as though the station inverted and it was Jake who dangled over the abyss and his father who stood on the edge of the platform, holding on to him with all his might.

The vision altered just as Jake felt his father's hand slip through his grasp. Jake watched in horror as his father spiralled down, down, into darkness.

The doors to the train sealed shut, and it began to roll. Jake pounded on the glass. He kicked at the doors, but it was too late. His father was gone.

CHAPTER FOURTEEN

Jake sank to his knees. "Stop the train." He pounded on the old doors until his fists were red and raw. "Stop …" But the station was long gone. The subway was already at top speed, winding through the black tunnel like a runaway freight. Jake finally gave up and collapsed to the floor. With his back against the doors, he closed his eyes.

Jake could sense the penetrating stares of the passengers. He could hear their wicked whispers echoing all around him. Still, he refused to look up. Even after he opened his eyes and wiped away his tears, he just sat there, gazing at his hand — the hand that had failed him, the hand that had let his father slip into oblivion.

"It's my fault. It's all my fault."

"What's your problem?" asked a familiar voice.

Short-Shorts stood in front of Jake, a huge grin plastered across his face. He looked different somehow. Jake hadn't remembered his eyes being quite so dark and sunken. The old pot lights lit his spiky hair, and Jake swore he could see patches of scalp.

"You got what you wanted, didn't you? You wanted to see your father and you did, right? So join the party. It's just getting started."

Jake gritted his teeth. "Who are you? And where am I?"

Short-Shorts seemed to find Jake's questions amusing. He glanced around at the others. "I'm nobody," he said. "*Mr.* Nobody to you." He laughed, and they all joined in — everyone except the girl who held her blanket and rocked back and forth, and the strange dark figure seated alone at the far end of the train. There was something familiar about that guy — his shape, his hair …

Short-Shorts bent down. He leaned in until he was face to face with Jake, the emptiness in his eyes hypnotically frightening. Then he spoke, and his words chilled Jake to the bone. "And you, dude, are nowhere."

Jake threw his whole weight forward and tackled the guy. They rolled on the floor, crashing toward the others, who sprang out of the way to clear a path. Jake was on top of Short-Shorts, pinning the guy on his stomach, pressing his face to the floor.

"What's going on here?" Jake screamed.

The other passengers formed a circle around them, jeering and laughing. Jake searched their faces. They were crazy. Every single one of them.

"What's wrong with all of you?" he yelled.

Beads of sweat formed on Jake's upper lip. Was it his imagination, or was the train getting warmer?

"Nothing's going on here," said Short-Shorts. "Absolutely nothing." Even under the circumstances, he wouldn't stop making cryptic jokes.

Jake searched the faces of those gathered around him. They were empty, hollow faces. Outnumbered by freaks, Jake let go of Short-Shorts. He took a deep breath and stood up. He could see the one guy still sitting all alone in the far corner of the train. Jake craned his neck to get a better look, but the crowd shifted inward, blocking his path.

"I don't know what this is all about," said Jake, focusing his attention on Short-Shorts, "and I don't even wanna know anymore. I just wanna go home. Can I go home now?"

The girl in the leopard-print pants stepped forward. "That's what we all want, Jakey-wakey. We all wanna go home."

"Yeah," said the guy in the leather jacket. "What makes you think you're so special?"

"Back off," said Short-Shorts. "Jake wants to go home …" He narrowed his eyes. "And why not?" he said finally. "Sounds like as good a plan as any …"

Before Jake could open his mouth to respond, the subway exploded into the station. The doors behind him slid open. Short-Shorts gave him a hard shove to the chest, sending him backward out the train. He landed on his back with a thud, smacking his head on the concrete platform.

CHAPTER FIFTEEN

When Jake opened his eyes, he was lying on his back on the southbound platform in St. George Station.

He sat up — an action that set the world spinning. His head throbbed. He reached up and felt a tennis ball–sized lump. Jake took a deep breath, and everything settled long enough for him to inspect his surroundings. Directly in front of him was the large ad with the grinning white-toothed people. The clock on the plasma screen read twelve o'clock. Had he returned home? Or had he never even left?

Jake's thoughts were soupy. It hurt to think. Before any of the craziness began he'd been running for the subway train and he'd missed it. Had he slipped in his attempt to catch the train? Had he fallen backward and hit his head? Had it all been some crazy concussion-induced fantasy?

He rolled onto all fours, then pushed himself to his feet. His legs trembled. His head was an overinflated balloon ready to pop. A smattering of people stood on the opposite platform, but no one was looking in his direction. Jake's side of the tracks was empty — except for the homeless guy, who had apparently decided to have a nap on one of the benches.

No point in asking him anything, Jake thought with a wry grin, though deep down he was relieved to see the man. He felt a twinge of sympathy, having recently experienced homelessness first-hand — or at least he thought he had.

Jake dug into his pocket and located his old transfer. His wallet, keys, iPod, and phone were there, as well. Jake shook his head and sighed — it had to have been a dream. There was no other explanation.

Stepping onto the escalator, Jake headed down toward the east–west line. He scrutinized every ad, every person, every bit of space, searching for anything unusual. Everything appeared normal — completely normal. But to be certain, Jake hit the transfer machine and drew out the small slip of paper. He took a long, drawn-out breath, then peered at the transfer. He was home!

Jake rubbed his head as the subway zipped back to Victoria Park Station. Once he got home, he'd put some ice on that lump. *Home.* What a wonderful word. He'd remember never to take it for granted again.

When Jake got on the bus, he flashed the driver his transfer. The man was reading a newspaper and didn't even look up. With the strangest feeling of déjà vu, Jake sat back and watched the houses and buildings melt away until he reached his stop. It was a huge relief to be holding his keys in his hands as he jogged up the side street toward his building.

Halfway there, Jake's phone vibrated. He pulled it out of his pocket. Happy to see the text, Jake forgot how angry he'd been at Cole.

Where are you, man? You're missing a wild party. Shelly's been asking for you.

Jake smiled. He stuffed the phone back into his pocket. He'd call Cole in the morning. No matter how wild Cole thought his party was, Jake was sure his had been wilder. Not even ten Shellys falling all over him could make him wish he was at that party. All he wanted right now was some ice for his head and the comfort of his warm bed.

Jake entered his building. Chipped paint, cracked walls, and graffiti greeted him. It felt so good to be home. He took the elevator up to the seventh floor, doing his best to ignore the uneasy feeling it still gave him. It was warm inside the elevator. Too warm. He was relieved when the doors slid open and he stepped out into the hallway.

Standing outside his apartment door, Jake ran his fingertips across the tarnished brass numbers — 710. Home, sweet home.

Jake placed his key in the door and gently turned until he heard the deadbolt click. He held his breath. The old hinges complained as the door slid open. He was sure his mom would pounce on him. When she didn't, a horrible memory streaked through his mind: that blood-shot eye, that crusty voice. For a second Jake's confidence faltered. Was he really home? Was his mother really there?

He crept toward the living room. Through the darkness he could make out her shape stretched across the sofa bed. Jake listened. Relief drizzled over him when he heard the familiar sound of her breathing. He closed his eyes and listened for several minutes. He'd missed her.

Jake walked to the kitchen and got some ice from the freezer. He wrapped it in a few sheets of paper towel and held it to his head. The coolness soothed his burning lump.

He stepped into his bedroom. There was no mistaking the familiar shape hidden beneath his brother's covers. Drew's breathing was raspy and annoying. Jake smiled. It was funny how all the little things that had bothered him were now strangely comforting.

Jake wanted to make as little noise as pos-sible, so he decided to hop into bed and sleep in his clothes. As he lay down, he held the ice

on his lump. It was much smaller already —
fading along with the weird dream. Once the
ice completely melted, Jake placed the wet
wad of tissue on his nightstand and closed his
eyes. Exhaustion overcame him, and he quickly
drifted off into a deep, deep sleep.

CHAPTER SIXTEEN

Jake rubbed his eyes and checked his alarm clock. It was a quarter past nine. Drew's bed was empty and already made. He must have just left. Drew had karate lessons at 9:30 on Saturday mornings and was pathologically punctual.

Sitting up, Jake stretched. His body was sore and stiff, but he felt strangely well rested. The events of the previous night were hazy in his mind, and now more than ever it all seemed like a bizarre nightmare. There were no crazy freaks riding some time train. He hadn't visited the past. He hadn't met his father.

Jake's head still ached, but as he ran a hand through his hair, he noticed the swelling had disappeared. He glanced at his nightstand. The wad of paper towels he'd left there the previous night was gone. Drew must have cleaned up. Aside from being pathologically punctual, his brother was obsessively neat. A mess would practically have to jump up and smack Jake across the face for him to do anything about it.

Swinging his legs over the edge of the bed, Jake suddenly remembered he'd slept in his clothes. He decided it would be a good idea to shower and put on something fresh before he faced his mother. Jake could hear her moving around in the kitchen, so he ducked into the bathroom quickly before she spotted him.

For the longest time Jake stood under the hot water, letting it wash away any trace of the previous night. When he was finished, he brushed his teeth and got dressed — opting for a fresh pair of jeans, a long-sleeved T-shirt, and his Kobe jersey.

There was buoyancy in his step as he entered the kitchen where his mother sat cradling a mug of coffee. She was gazing at the wall with vacant eyes, the way she did when she was really upset — beyond-words upset.

Oh-oh, Jake thought. *This can't be good.* Maybe she knew he'd been out. But then again, maybe she didn't. It was hard to tell. She had worked double shifts the previous week. She could just as easily be beyond-words exhausted. Jake decided it was best to play it cool. He'd gauge his situation by her response.

"Hey," he said in his most cheerful voice, strolling toward the fridge. He opened it, got out a carton of milk, and turned to face his mother.

His mother didn't react. She just sat there, perfectly still, staring at the wall, as though she were made of stone.

Quick. Say something. Anything.

"Where's Drew?" he asked, getting a glass from the cupboard and pouring himself some milk. He knew the answer, but it was the first thing that had popped into his mind. Jake took a huge gulp and let the cold liquid run down his throat. He sat down beside her. She didn't even glance in his direction.

The silent treatment. It could mean only one thing. She definitely knew he'd snuck out. Now, just like the last time, she was going to spend an entire week acting as if he didn't exist. The milk started to sour in Jake's stomach. Then he had a thought: maybe he should come clean. Maybe if he told her the truth she'd forgive him quicker.

Jake set his glass down on the table. "Okay, Mom, I know you know I snuck out. But I just wanted to go to a party. Is that so horrible?"

Still no response.

Jake leaned back in his chair. If he could just tell her everything. If she only knew how awful his experience had actually been, she'd know he'd been punished enough. But there was no way he could tell her. She'd never believe it. She'd think he was lying for sure, and then he'd wind up in worse trouble.

"If it makes you happy, I didn't even go," he offered. "I just turned around and came home. I swear."

Jake's mother closed her eyes. She took a deep breath and released the air slowly. When she opened her eyes, they were brimming with tears and her lower lip quivered. Jake felt terrible. He hated seeing her so sad. He reached over and almost put his hand on hers, but pulled back when she spoke.

"Why, Jake? Why would you do this to me?" The tears spilled over and streamed in rivulets down her cheeks.

"I just —" he began, but she cut him off.

"How could you take off like that? How could you just leave without saying anything?"

"I'm sorry —" he tried, but she interrupted again.

"What am I going to tell Drew?"

Jake was puzzled. "Drew? What's he got to do with —"

"I can't take it," she said. Her head dropped into her hands as she leaned forward on the table. She nearly knocked over her coffee cup. It wobbled, but Jake grabbed it and steadied it. "I can't live through this again," she said, sobbing. "Not again. Not you, too …"

Why was she so upset? What was she talking about? Jake struggled to understand. *You, too?* What did she mean by *too?*

Then it dawned on him. This wasn't about the party at all. This wasn't about the fact that he'd snuck out for the night. This was about something entirely different. He'd up and left. Snuck out without telling her. His father had up and left — maybe without telling her. It all started to make sense. In her mind Jake had done the same thing. It must have been like ripping apart an old wound. He'd been so focused on himself that he hadn't thought about what finding him missing would mean to her.

"It's okay, Mom," Jake said. "I'm here now, and I won't do it again. I promise. I'll never leave without telling you."

She sobbed even louder, as if she hadn't heard a word he'd said. He couldn't understand it. Jake apologized again, but it was as though nothing he could say could possibly make up for what he'd done. He wanted her to stop crying. It was killing him, but he didn't know what else to say. Maybe she just needed to get it out of her system. Maybe she just needed some space.

Jake stood up. "I'm gonna go to my room, okay?" When she didn't reply, he added quickly, "I think I have some homework I need to work on ... and ... I think I'll straighten up a bit, too."

There. If that didn't make her happy, nothing would.

He lingered a moment longer. She stopped crying and resumed staring at the wall. Jake sighed and turned to leave the kitchen. A week's worth of the silent treatment would be tough to take.

Even if the previous night had been nothing but a dream, it had been so nice to see his mother standing on that porch happy for a change. Seeing her looking so cheerful was almost worth all the other freaky stuff he'd gone through. Almost.

Before he left he turned to grab his glass of milk from the table. It wasn't there.

CHAPTER SEVENTEEN

Jake's phone vibrated. "Hey," he said. "I was just going to call —"

"Jake? Yo, Jake, you there?" It was Cole, and he sounded pretty stoked, given the fact that he'd probably partied all night.

"I'm here. What's up?"

"Jake, can you hear me? You there?"

There was something wrong with the line. Cole's voice came through loud and clear, but apparently Jake's voice was lost in cyberspace. Sometimes reception in the old building wasn't good. Jake got out of bed and walked toward his bedroom door. "Can you hear me now?"

Empty space. The line crackled and then went dead. Jake examined his phone. He was confused when he saw that he had tons of missed calls. Jake was about to check his messages when his phone buzzed again. Cole had sent him a text.

What's up, man? Where have you been?

Jake responded. *Just chillin'. What's doing?*

What's wrong with your phone? I just tried calling you.

Bad reception.

You missed a hot party. Can't believe you were a no-show. Loser.

Cole never missed an opportunity to put Jake down. Jake hated to admit it, but sometimes he wondered whether his mother was right about Cole. Maybe the guy wasn't such a good friend, after all.

There was no point in even trying to explain to Cole that he'd actually gone to the party, missed it, bumped his head, and slipped into the Twilight Zone. Jake's thumbs zipped across the keys. *Got the text too late.*

Sure. Whatever. Meet me at the coffee shop. I need to talk to you.

Jake knew exactly what Cole wanted to talk about. He was going to try to convince Jake to go with him tomorrow to make Vlad's delivery. He was all super-bad on the outside, but inside Cole was poultry. He'd be too afraid to go it alone. Jake was about to tell Cole to relax, that he'd made up his mind and was definitely going along, but after that loser comment, he decided to let his friend sweat a bit. He'd tell him in person.

See you in ten.

Jake stepped into the hall. He could hear the water running in the bathtub. He knocked on the door but got no response, so he knocked again and shouted, "I'm going to meet Cole for a coffee. You want a doughnut or something?"

Jake waited a few seconds. He thought he heard her say something like, "Come home ..."

He rolled his eyes and quickly added, "I'll only be gone for an hour or so."

Nothing.

Given the choice, Jake would take his mother whaling on him any day over the silent treatment. Funny thing was, this wasn't exactly the silent treatment. It was more like the *selective* silent treatment.

Jake gave up trying to figure her out and left the apartment. As he rode the elevator, his eyes circled from the ceiling to the wall to the floor and back again. He didn't hear any more voices, but he could have sworn it was five thousand degrees inside the tiny space. There was something wrong with it — he'd have to remember to tell Mr. Borrelli next time he saw him. If the elevator had some sort of electrical problem, someone could get seriously hurt.

By the time Jake reached the lobby, he was dripping with sweat. He swiped his hand across his forehead as the doors opened. Two men waited to get on, neither too interested in clearing a path for him. Jake had to squeeze between the two guys to get out while they muscled past him to get on. They were like pillars of stone, practically knocking him down all the while continuing their conversation.

Jake shook his head. "Bunch of ignorant ..." he muttered under his breath, but the doors were already closing.

Jake stepped out of the building and into the cool fall air. He stood for a moment and scanned his neighbourhood. It wasn't such a bad place, after all. He was about to head to the coffee shop when he saw Mr. Borrelli walking toward his car.

"Yo, Mr. B!" he shouted, but the superintendent didn't hear him. "Hold up, Mr. B!" Jake tried again, jogging toward the parking lot. Mr. Borrelli got into his car. The Toyota backed up and then sped toward the main road so fast that Jake had to dive out of the way to avoid getting hit.

What is it with everybody? he thought, shaking his head. He shrugged. Ah, well, he'd have to tell Mr. Borrelli about the elevator another time.

As Jake made his way to the coffee shop, he passed house after house all decked out with ghosts and scarecrows and pumpkins for Halloween. Drew would be going trick-or-treating soon. His brother was really excited. He was dressing up as the Grim Reaper, wearing their mother's old black hooded poncho and carrying a scythe he'd made out of a broomstick and cardboard wrapped in aluminum foil. Jake had given him the idea. Drew did whatever

Jake told him to do. He'd given Jake all his money without question when Jake had asked. His mother was right. Drew looked up to him. Jake suddenly felt pretty bad about taking advantage of his little brother. He sucked in a lungful of crisp autumn air and picked up his pace. Vlad would probably toss Cole and him a few bucks after they made the delivery — that way Jake could give Drew back all the money he'd taken from him and maybe even some interest.

When Jake arrived at the coffee shop, he stood outside, peering through the grimy window. He could see the woman behind the counter. She was filling sugar containers. He'd never paid her much attention in the past, but now he found his eyes drawn to her. Although she looked a lot older, she was definitely the same woman he'd encountered in his dream — the one who had given him the phone book, the one who had called the police. Jake put his hand on the door, then hesitated. For a second he wondered whether she'd recognize him and call the police again. *That's dumb*, he told himself. *It was all a dream. It never happened.* He pushed open the door and stepped inside.

Cole sat at their usual table, scarfing down a chocolate doughnut and fiddling with his phone. He was always playing games, so intense, as if he were five years old. He'd be all happy when he won and all sulky when he messed up. He got really mad if anyone interrupted him and made him blow his game.

Jake sat in front of Cole, who ignored him and kept on playing.

"Booyah!" said Cole, clicking like crazy.

Obviously, he was doing well. Jake frowned. This game might go on forever.

"S'up, man?" Jake said, deciding he'd take his chances, but Cole was too focused to respond. Jake rolled his eyes. "Relax. It's just a game. The way you act, you'd think it was rocket science."

"Let's go … bring it on, baby … bring it on …"

"Cole. Dude. I thought you wanted to see me?"

Cole clicked away, oblivious to the world around him. Jake sighed and waited, once again wondering whether his mother had Cole pegged for the selfish person he was.

Suddenly, Cole slammed his phone on the table so hard that Jake was sure the thing would smash into a million pieces.

"You're an idiot, you know that?" said Jake.

Cole glanced up. Looked directly at Jake. He didn't say a word — as if he were peering through him.

CHAPTER EIGHTEEN

Jake waved a hand in front of Cole's face. The guy didn't flinch. Instead, Cole looked away. He glanced at the door, as though he was expecting someone to walk in any second.

"Cole, quit messin' with me. Say something."

No response.

Something wasn't right. Jake's heart shifted into overdrive. He could feel it revving in his chest.

Cole picked up his phone and checked the time. He gazed at the door again.

"Cole!" Jake shouted. "What's your problem? Talk to me, man!"

Cole's thumbs danced across the keys on his phone. Was he going to play another game?

"What are you doing?" demanded Jake, his pitch rising as panic grabbed his throat and squeezed.

In that same second Jake's phone buzzed. He froze, his eyes widening like canyons. With trembling hands he pulled the cell out of his pocket and peered at the screen. Jake's knees buckled. The coffee shop began to spin. Cole had sent him a text.

What's taking you?

Jake gulped down the bitterness that rose into his throat. He found his voice but managed only a thin whisper. "If this is your idea of a joke, it's not funny."

Cole placed his phone on the table. He glanced at the door once more, then leaned back in his chair and yawned.

The world around Jake cracked and crumbled. Either Cole was messing with his mind or ...

No! Jake squeezed the thought into an iron box in his mind and bolted it shut, but it forced its way back out. His mother wasn't talking to him. The guys in the elevator didn't see him. Mr. Borrelli nearly ran him over.

Standing up, Jake took a step backward. *No,* he told himself. He refused to let his mind go there. Instead, Jake moved toward Cole and grabbed the guy's shoulder. He could feel it — the bone, the flesh, the muscle. Cole was real. But Cole didn't move. He didn't seem to feel Jake's hand. He didn't seem to see Jake. How was that possible?

Jake tried to shove Cole, but he couldn't budge him. He threw his whole weight forward, both hands pushing as hard as he could against Cole's back, but Cole was a cast-iron statue.

Cole reached forward and picked up his doughnut. Jake tried to stop him. He tried to yank his arm down, but it was impossible. It was as if they were both made of totally different substances, completely different matter. Or maybe different states of matter, as if Cole were solid and Jake were gas. Or maybe they existed in entirely separate dimensions. Alternate realities.

Losing it, Jake balled his fist and punched Cole's shoulder as hard as he could. A searing pain raced through his knuckles, as if he'd just struck a tank. Cole went on eating, though, oblivious to Jake's attempts to reach him.

Jake screamed at the top of his lungs, "What's happening to me?" He spun around and around, but no one in the coffee shop took any notice of him. Not Cole. Not the lady behind the counter. None of the other customers. Jake gripped his head with both hands, pressing hard against his skull, squeezing his eyes shut.

Not again ...

Then he heard Short-Shorts' words drifting toward him from some distant past: *You can get off, Jake ... but you can't leave.* And suddenly Jake was plummeting backward down a deep, dark shaft, falling ... falling ...

"This isn't happening!" he cried.

He grabbed hold of the nearest table, opened his eyes, and steadied himself. If he wasn't really here, then where was he? Jake didn't even know what the word *real* meant anymore. Maybe he was real, and Cole and everyone else in the coffee shop were visions or ghosts. Maybe Short-Shorts had drugged him, or hypnotized him ... or ...

He had to figure this out. Then an idea struck him like a fist.

Jake raced toward the counter and leaped over it. He searched underneath until he found the phone book. It was older, practically falling apart, but Jake recognized the scribbled numbers, the doodle of the two hearts — it was the same book. He flipped frantically through the pages. Ma, Mabley, MacArthur, Mackinnon ...

The next page had been torn out.

Jake shut his eyes. Questions crashed like waves on the shore of his consciousness. Had it really happened? Had he visited the past? Had he dragged his father into his own nightmare? Was that where he had disappeared to all those years ago? Where was his father now? And what did the word *now* mean, anyway?

Opening his eyes, Jake looked up. An eerie calm settled over him. He stared blankly ahead until his eyes focused on his reflection in the glass door. He wasn't wearing his Kobe jersey. He was back in his black hoodie — the same black hoodie he'd worn the previous night.

The party wasn't over.

CHAPTER NINETEEN

Jake left the coffee shop in a zombie-like trance. He practically walked right into Damon. Jake sidestepped him, barely registering his presence. He kept on moving straight ahead until he reached the curb. The cool fall breeze numbed his face, lifting the fine hairs on the back of his neck as he watched the cars race by.

If he was a ghost, could a car hit him? *Kill* him? In the messed-up state of mind he was in he almost walked out into traffic just to see what would happen. He put one foot forward and stopped.

Jake rubbed his knuckles against his thigh. They still stung from punching Cole. Whether he was real or not the pain sure was. Jake could definitely feel things and couldn't pass through walls or doors. He had even needed a key to get into his apartment. Jake had to get control of himself. Taking a long breath, he drew in his foot.

There was only one thing he was certain about: if there was a way out of this nightmare, he'd find it at St. George Station. He had to get back there. He had to get back on that train.

Jake's phone vibrated. He'd forgotten that somehow the piece of technology was his only link to the real world. It vibrated a second time, and Jake checked it. Cole had sent him a text.

Don't bother coming. I'm outta here.

Jake turned to face the shop and waited. He expected to see his buddy come strolling out of the door. He didn't. Several minutes passed and still no Cole. What was going on? Then it occurred to Jake that Damon was inside the coffee shop, as well. Peering through the window, he saw Cole and Damon sitting together, coffees in hand, no indication of either being even remotely ready to leave. Why would Cole tell him not to bother coming? Why would he say he was leaving when he wasn't?

Opening the door, he slipped inside. As he approached their table, he watched Cole slide a huge wad of bills over to Damon, who took the cash and stuffed it into his pocket.

Jake lowered himself gently into an empty seat next to them. Where would Cole get that much money? And why was he giving it to Damon? Jake began wondering what else Cole was mixed up in.

"I'm telling you, he'll show," Cole said. He started chewing his lip.

Damon scowled. "Make sure. He's been on the fence long enough. Time to give him a shove." His mouth curled into a thin grin, but his eyes were unsmiling. "And you know what could happen to *you* if he doesn't show."

Jake tried to keep up with the conversation, but it was as if they were tap dancing and he was a few beats behind.

"When you go in, make sure he's holding the bag," said Damon. "That way, if anyone has to go down, it won't be you. Get it?"

"Sure," said Cole. He shifted his eyes to the door as though he was worried Jake might turn up, after all. "No worries. He'll do what I tell him."

Who was Cole talking about? Could Cole possibly mean Jake? One thing was certain — they were discussing the delivery. Like the pieces of some intricate puzzle, things were starting to fall into place, and Jake didn't like the picture that was forming.

"He's got a little brother, right?" said Damon, his grey eyes cold and lifeless.

Jake sprang to his feet. "Leave Drew outta this!" He was about to take a shot at Damon, tell him Vlad could take his delivery and go to hell, but then he remembered he was only half there.

"Drew?" asked Cole. "What's his kid brother got to do with anything?"

"Insurance," said Damon. He grinned, and his resemblance to Vlad was more pronounced.

"If MacRae doesn't show, use his brother. Either way, you stay clean. You can get to him, can't you?"

Anger ripped through Jake's body. He snatched Damon's cup and whipped it across the room. Coffee splashed all over the floor. Jake blinked, and the mess was gone. The coffee cup was back on the table in front of Damon, as if he hadn't laid a hand on it.

"I ... I dunno." Cole's voice cracked. Damon narrowed his eyes, and Cole added quickly, "I guess so. Leave it with me."

Powerlessness fuelled Jake's rage. He paced the floor like a tiger in a cage. He heard everything, was watching it all go down, and yet he couldn't do a thing to stop it.

Jake froze. Where had he heard that before? His mind raced. Hadn't his mother said almost the exact same thing to Jake just last night?

"Send me a text tomorrow if Jake shows up or if you've got the kid," said Damon. "I'll take it from there." He stood up, took a last gulp of coffee, scrunched the paper cup, and tossed it onto the table. Then he patted Cole on the shoulder and swaggered toward the door.

Cole sat quietly like an obedient dog that had been told to stay. Jake stared at him, venom seeping from every pore in his body. Four years of friendship and Jake didn't have a clue who

Cole really was — or what he was capable of. How could Jake have been so blind? Cole was setting him up to take the fall, just so he could stay clean. Just so the 5 Kings would think he was a hotshot. Jake's mother had been right all along. Why hadn't he listened to her? The worst kind of enemy was the one disguised as a friend.

Picking up his phone, Cole punched out Jake's home number. Drew would be coming home any second now.

Jake was frantic. He tried to rip the cell out of Cole's hand, but he couldn't budge it. He punched Cole again — this time harder. Jake's knuckles were on fire, but Cole just sat there calmly, listening to the phone ring.

I've gotta find a way to break through, Jake told himself. *I've gotta contact Drew before Cole gets to him ... but how?*

He could text him — that would work. Only Drew didn't have a phone. He could call him on the landline, but just like Cole, Drew wouldn't be able to hear his voice. Jake was out of his mind. He had to do something — anything. He had to stop Cole.

"Hello?"

Jake recognized his brother's voice.

Cole stood up, his voice smooth as silk. "What up, Drewster?"

CHAPTER TWENTY

Jake sprinted all the way back to his apartment. He punched the elevator button three or four times, but it was taking too long, so he took the stairs. He raced up flight after flight until he burst through the metal door and into the hallway.

Fumbling for his keys, Jake managed to unlock the door. He threw it open and charged inside. Voices were coming from the kitchen. He bolted toward them. Drew and his mom were sitting at the table. Drew was still wearing his karate gi — he was already a black belt.

Jake steadied himself against the wall, downing huge gulps of air. How would he get a message to Drew? What could he do?

"I don't get it," said Drew. "Where would he go? And why wouldn't he say anything?"

Jake's mother closed her eyes. Her whole body seemed to droop, beginning with her chin and rippling down her body. She lifted her head, opened her mouth to speak, but no words came out.

"Call him!" Drew said. "Call his cell!" He stood up. "*I'm* gonna call!"

She grabbed his hand and pulled him back down. "It's no use. I've tried calling. All morning. He's not answering."

Jake checked his phone. The missed calls!

"Can't you do anything?" Drew pleaded. "Can't you call the police?"

Jake's mother slowly shook her head, her voice apologetic. "Already tried that. They have an Amber Alert out. About as much as they'll do."

"*Why*? Why aren't they out looking for him?"

Frustration rose in her voice. "Jake's taken off before, that's why. They don't take you seriously when you've called before insisting your kid has been kidnapped and then he strolls in the next morning, half-drunk from his wild night of partying. The police just think he's a dumb teenager. A writeoff. They're not looking for him. They've got better things to do."

The words were like a bucket of ice water thrown in his face. *A dumb teenager? A writeoff?* Jake shook his head. Okay, so he wasn't exactly a *model* kid. He'd made some bad decisions, but nothing major. And now, if he couldn't find a way out of this nightmare, that was all they'd think of him — a dumb runaway. Some legacy.

Drew's lip began to tremble. He was fighting back tears. Jake hated himself. He shouldn't be putting his brother through this.

Jake's mom got up and hugged Drew. "Don't worry," she whispered. "He'll be back. He will."

Jake wanted to hug her — to hug both of them. He took a step toward them.

"I just talked to Cole," Drew said, sniffling.

Jake's spine straightened.

"He asked if I knew where Jake was. He said Jake was supposed to meet him and didn't show."

"What else did he say?" asked Jake, but Drew didn't hear. Jake paced the floor. He had to know what Cole was planning if he was going to find a way to protect his brother.

Jake's mother got up. She went to the counter to get a tissue. "I spoke to Cole earlier. He's got no idea where Jake is."

"Cole said," Drew muttered, "if I just … he wants me to …" His voice trailed off.

What? What did he say? What does he want you to do? Jake moved toward his brother. He put his hands on Drew's shoulders. Drew sat perfectly still. He didn't feel a thing.

"What's that?" said his mother, approaching with a wad of tissues.

Drew took them mechanically. He swiped them across his nose and placed them on the table. "Um … nothing," he said, avoiding her eyes.

Tell her, Drew! Tell her what Cole wants you to do! Jake's stomach churned. How could he break through? How could he make Drew understand that something bad was going down and that he needed to stay away from Cole?

Jake picked up a chair and hurled it across the kitchen. It smashed against the wall. Then, like that, it was right back beside Jake. He tried to grab Drew and shake him. He pushed and pulled and heaved, but he couldn't move him. Not one inch. He grabbed a pen from the counter and gouged his name in huge block letters into the kitchen wall, but as soon as he finished, the wall was clean again.

Jake dug into his pocket and pulled out his phone. He called his home number. The phone rang instantly. It startled both Drew and his mother. They raced toward the counter, his mother taking the call.

"Hello?" she said.

"It's me! It's Jake! I'm here in the room right beside you!"

"Jake? Jake, is that you?"

For a second Jake actually thought she'd heard him. "Yeah, it's me! It's me, Mom!"

"Jake? Jake, if it's you, say something. Please!"

Tears streamed down his mother's cheeks, and it became clear that she couldn't hear him.

Drew grabbed the phone. "Jake, where are you? Come home! Please come home!"

Jake slammed his phone down on the table. He collapsed into the chair he had hurled across the room a moment before and watched as his mother and brother heard the line go dead. They looked at each other, and though no words were spoken, Jake knew the message passing between them. Jake's call had only made things worse. Tears filled with anger and frustration spilled down his cheeks. He swiped at them bitterly.

Trapped in his non-existence, he was wasting time. There was nothing he could do here. He couldn't help his brother like this. There was only one way out. Only one way to change things. Jake had to get back on that subway train.

CHAPTER TWENTY-ONE

Crouched in a corner of St. George Station with his back against the wall, Jake watched and waited. Time trickled like a leaky faucet. Every muscle, every nerve, was tight with anticipation. It took all his energy to remain still as trains arrived and departed.

As a kid, Jake had always thought it would be really cool to be invisible — like a superhero, able to sneak around unnoticed and do whatever he pleased. But now here he was, observing people go about their business, not one of them with even an inkling that he existed, and it was the worst feeling in the world.

What if the train never came back? What if he was stuck in this freaky limbo forever? He shook his head. No. The train was coming. Although he hadn't the foggiest idea as to how or why, he was connected to it, and it was strangely comforting knowing that he'd be back on it soon.

"Almost …"

Someone had spoken! Jake glanced up out of reflex. He'd resigned himself to the fact that he was a ghost. It didn't even occur to Jake that he could be seen by a living soul.

"Salvation is at hand ..."

Jake's gaze settled on the leathery face, the ragged clothing, and the matted hair of the figure looming over him. A surge of shock rippled through his body.

"You can *s-see* me?" he stammered, scrambling to his feet.

"Darkness surrounds us ..." said the homeless man, his arms stretched wide. "Can you see it? Can you see through it?"

A jumble of emotions squirmed inside Jake. Someone was talking to him. Someone could see him. Did that mean Jake was real? Or did it mean that the homeless guy was a ghost, too? Jake reached out and touched the man's shoulders. His fingers slid over the greasy material.

"What's going on? What's happening to me?"

The man took a step back. He slipped out of Jake's grasp like water through a sieve. He shook his head. "You can't unspill milk."

"What does that mean?" Jake demanded. "Stop talking in riddles!"

A train pulled into the station. The clock read 11:59.

"Life is a riddle," said the man. "You can spend your whole life trying to figure it out ..."

The chimes rang through the station, and the doors sealed shut. The platform was empty, and the train began to roll.

"Don't give me that crap!" cried Jake. "Tell me the truth. I need to know."

As the last car passed, Jake checked the clock. It was exactly noon. Ribbons of black smoke snaked out of the tunnel opening at the far end of the station. Jake's eyes grew wide. For a second he thought there was a fire in the tunnel, but no one else on the platform reacted. The ground shuttered. It was coming.

Jake turned back to face the homeless man. He was about to demand answers when he saw something in the man's eyes that forced him to take a step back. "Who are you?"

Smoke billowed from the opening, and a low rumble shook the ceiling and floor.

"I ... I don't know," said the homeless man. His clouded eyes searched the air for answers.

Just then the maroon train exploded through the tunnel with a thunderous roar. It flew toward Jake like some prehistoric beast.

"I ... I'm not sure anymore," mumbled the homeless man. The train screeched to a halt, and the doors flew open. "I'm lost. I've lost everything ..."

Including your mind, thought Jake. Still, he wanted to hear what the man had to say. But there was no time; he had to leave. He had to save Drew. Jake stepped inside the subway car.

"I've fallen from grace," said the man. "I'm falling ..."

The doors closed in front of Jake. He watched as the strange man scratched his head and gazed at the empty platform. Then the train plunged into darkness and the vision was gone.

CHAPTER TWENTY-TWO

"What took you so long?"

The dim lights flickered. Music played. The same creepy characters stood around the subway car talking and laughing. It was a party that went on forever.

Jake sucked in a lungful of stale air. He stared long and hard at Short-Shorts, certain the guy had less hair. It was as though someone had ripped out clumps of it, exposing patches of scalp. His eyes were sunken and bloodshot, and his skin seemed different, too — all blotchy and full of lesions. The sweatbands he wore around his wrists had deep brownish-red stains.

"What kind of weird place is this? Why am I here?"

"Relax. It's like I told you," said Short-Shorts. "You're one of the lucky ones." He grinned, revealing yellow rotting teeth.

Jake took a step toward him. "I'm stuck in this nightmare with you freaks and you call me *lucky*?" His voice echoed through the subway car.

Everyone stopped talking and turned to face Jake — everyone except the girl rocking back and forth, hugging her little baby blanket, and the lone, dark figure sitting at the back of the train.

Jake stared at them. Like Short-Shorts, they all appeared different, as though they had some type of flesh-eating disease. Jake backed up slowly until he was against the doors. "Just tell me how to get back to reality. I need to get back. Not for me — for my brother."

Short-Shorts glanced around at the other passengers. A silent message passed between them. Then he looked Jake straight in the eye. "I dunno ... life's a series of choices. You've already made some pretty bad ones ..."

Jake's mind skipped like a stone across a muddy pond. His English teacher, Mr. Dean, had talked about choices. His mother had talked about choices. And now Short-Shorts ...

"What have my choices got to do with all this?" Jake asked Short-Shorts.

"They've got everything to do with everything. Make your choice. Live with the consequences."

"Whatever," said Jake, shaking his head.

So he liked to gamble. So he had a loser friend, Cole. And he was mixed up with Damon, Vlad, and the 5 Kings. But this guy was talking to him as if he'd robbed a bank — or worse.

"Just tell me what I need to do to get off this ride for good. Back to my life. My *real* life — not some bizarre alternate universe. Whatever you want me to do, I'll do it. I swear."

Short-Shorts shook his head. "It's not that easy." He leaned in and whispered in Jake's ear, "You've got another stop."

The guy's breath was hot and rancid. Bile rose in Jake's throat. He pressed his back against the doors, but they gave way and he was falling backward.

CHAPTER TWENTY-THREE

Jake stood on the platform in St. George Station once again, only this time he held no illusions — he wasn't home. A strange calmness settled over him as he watched the train disappear into the tunnel. It would be back.

He glanced at the flat screen and nodded — exactly twelve. But was it noon on Saturday, or midnight on Friday, or another twelve o'clock altogether? Somehow Jake had lost all sense of time. Hunger, thirst, exhaustion — they'd all evaporated. He felt nothing but a dull, aching emptiness swelling inside him.

Jake rubbed his eyes and ran both hands through his hair. He had to stay calm.

The opposite side of the tracks was packed with people, including young children, which told Jake it was most likely noon. Only a few stragglers meandered about on his side; obviously a train had recently come and gone.

Jake's eyes darted from one advertisement to another. He didn't recognize a single image. Scaffolding was set up at the far end of the platform, and a few workers were chiselling off the old tiles. Everything had changed once again.

He found himself wishing the homeless man would appear, but the guy was nowhere to be found. As Jake stood there contemplating his surroundings, a shiver crawled up his spine. What new reality had he stepped into?

On his way to the escalator, Jake passed the workers. "You, uh, got the time?" He swallowed. His voice sounded strange. Hollow.

"Check the screen," one man grunted. He didn't even turn to look at Jake; he just kept on hammering away at the stubborn old tiles.

At least I'm not a ghost, thought Jake. It was a minor relief.

As he rode the escalator downward, he checked his pockets. Everything was there: his wallet, cellphone, iPod, and keys. He should be calling home, but there was no point. He wouldn't get very good reception in the tunnels. He had to get to Drew as quickly as he could. He could still hear his brother's conversation with Cole echoing in his mind.

The memory spurred Jake into motion. He sprinted through the station toward the east–west line where a subway had just arrived. Jumping on before the doors closed, he rode all the way to Victoria Park Station before realizing he hadn't taken a transfer slip.

Jake groped around in his pocket and located his stray change. If he was lucky, it would be enough to pay his fare. Then he felt something else hidden deep in his pocket. Gingerly, he withdrew the mass. The transfer that should have been brand-new looked ancient. Jake sighed. He had given up trying to make sense of the absurd. All logic and reason had gone packing long ago. Pressing everything else from his mind, he zeroed in on one thought — Drew.

Jumping off the train, Jake took the escalator up into the busy station. The walls were now clad in stainless steel from floor to ceiling. The ticket booth was made of seamless glass. There were no transfer machines in sight, and the old turnstiles were replaced with archways that looked more like metal detectors.

For a second Jake wondered where he was, but engraved into the metal walls in bold block letters were the words: VICTORIA PARK.

Jake gave his head a shake. *Drew*. His brother was all that mattered.

He raced through the metal archways toward the buses. The terminal had been renovated, as well, but Jake barely took any notice. He took the stairs two at a time and hopped onto the waiting bus.

The bus driver glanced up from the e-book he was reading. He frowned and motioned his chin to a flat panel where the fare box should have been. It had an outline of a hand.

Jake stared at the shape, then realized it was a scanner. Hesitating for a moment, he placed his hand on it. A buzzer sounded, and the driver looked up again, this time decidedly annoyed. Jake put his hand on the scanner again, but the buzzer went off a second time.

"Where'd you get on?" demanded the bus driver.

"St. George," Jake said, though he wasn't sure anymore. It was all a blur. A never-ending journey aboard the public transit system.

"St. George?" the man grumbled. "Didn't you scan your palm when you paid your fare?"

"Um, yeah, sure," Jake lied.

The driver put his e-book aside and fixed Jake with a suspicious stare. "You sure about that? Or maybe you snuck on between the crowds?"

Jake opened his mouth to lie again, but the driver cut him off. He pointed to a poster hanging above the driver's seat — NO PALM. NO PASSAGE. "Afraid you gotta pay another ten-fifty, son," he said.

Ten-fifty? This guy was out of his mind. You would need a mortgage to pay that fare. Jake didn't even have a third of that. How was he going to get home? It would take him forever to walk. He reached into his pocket and pulled out his change, including the wrinkled old transfer slip.

The bus driver's eyes widened. "Where'd you dig *that* up?" he asked. "Haven't seen one of those in years."

Years? thought Jake, handing the driver the fragile slip of paper.

A smile slid over the man's lips. "I used to collect these back when I was a kid." The driver glanced over his shoulder, checking to see if anyone was watching. "Go ahead." He handed back the paper and jerked his chin toward the back of the bus. "Make sure you scan your palm next time."

Confused but grateful, Jake accepted the free ride and moved to the rear of the bus. He sat down just as the vehicle lurched forward, rolling out of the dark tunnel and into the bright light of day.

Drew. He'd call his brother now. Jake leaned back into the cool leather seat and pulled out his phone. The date glared at him from the tiny screen — the day and month, but not the year. He was about to call Drew when he paused. Jake had to know for sure. He opened the calendar. The phone quivered in his hands.

CHAPTER TWENTY-FOUR

Jake stood outside his apartment building examining the cracked, graffitied walls. Cool air swirled round him in a tornado of litter and leaves. Were they still living there? Was *he* still living there?

He had interfered with the past with disastrous results. Now here he stood, ten years into his future, wondering if he should risk meddling with it, too. Was it even possible to meddle with something that technically hadn't happened yet?

Jake took a deep breath. Whatever danger Drew had been in with Cole, it was long gone — over a whole decade ago. Wasn't it?

This is no accident, Jake's gut told him. *That train brought me here for a reason.*

He swallowed what saliva he could muster and reached into his pocket for his keys. As he was about to enter through the main doors, a woman approached and tapped a card to a scanner where the keyhole should have been. Jake knew this technology. He'd seen it before — though he never imagined it would find its way to his low-rent building. Jake moved quickly, ducking inside right behind her.

The old foyer looked pretty much the same — only ten years more rundown than the last time he'd seen it. He approached the elevators and hit the button. When the doors slid open, Jake did a double take. The interior of the elevator had been completely redone. He sighed. *At least they fixed one thing in this rat hole.*

Jake let the woman get on first. She was dressed in familiar jeans and a huge T-shirt, but nothing registered until she turned and looked right at Jake. It was his mother!

Startled by her appearance, he put a hand out to steady himself. Her hair was almost completely grey. It hung limp along her sallow cheeks. Her eyes were glazed, and a vacant smile caressed her lips.

"Mom?" whispered Jake.

Her expression remained blank. She stared past him as if he blended into the floral wallpaper. Jake's pulse quickened. Was he a ghost again?

"It's me, Mom," he said softly, moving closer to her. His lip began to tremble and his voice cracked. "It's Jake."

"Jake, fake, lake, cake … how many words rhyme with Jake?" She giggled like a second-grade girl and wound a strand of hair around her index finger.

It frightened Jake. He frowned, struggling to understand. This was his mother. She was here and she was real. But it wasn't her. She wasn't complete. There was something missing.

"Mom, look at me — I'm Jake. I'm your son!"

"Sunshine on my shoulders makes me happy …" she sang. *"I'm walkin' on sunshine …"*

"Stop it!" he cried. "Stop it!" He grabbed her arm. Her smile evaporated and her glossy eyes widened. "It's me," he said, tightening his grip. "Your son."

"You are my sunshine, my only sunshine …" Her voice was high-pitched and trembling as she struggled to break free from his grasp.

"Come on," he cried frantically, tears filling his eyes. "You know me!"

She stopped struggling as if seeing him for the first time. In a fleeting moment of lucidity she reached out her finger and caught a tear before it spilled down his cheek. "Jake?" she whispered, her voice like the flutter of a butterfly's wings.

Then, as quickly as it came, the clarity departed and the vacant expression returned to her eyes. She slipped gently from his grasp. "You should wear boots today. The weather man says it might snow."

Jake swiped at his face. He swallowed the salty phlegm that had gathered at the back of his throat. What was wrong with her?

The doors to the elevator opened. She turned and exited, humming to herself. Jake followed.

"Where's Drew?" he whispered.

She stopped short. Her spine straightened. She turned to face Jake, her brow furled as though she were calculating a difficult math problem. "Do I know Drew? Maybe I do ..." She exploded in giggles at her inadvertent rhyme.

Jake shut his eyes. He wanted to scream ... to hit something. He needed answers, and clearly his poor mother had none to give. Jake watched her open the apartment door, humming again mindlessly.

"I'll talk to Mr. Borrelli," Jake said aloud. "He'll know where Drew is."

His mother stopped humming. "Borrelli ..." she muttered as if reaching back into the darkest corner of her mind. "Borrelli's gone. Went to jail years ago."

"J-Jail?" Jake stuttered. If there was any doubt in him before, he now knew for certain that she had gone completely mad.

"Criminal negligence causing death," said his mother in a sinister tone. "She died, you know. He should have checked the wiring. It was his responsibility. That's what the prosecutor said."

What in the world was she going on about? *Criminal negligence causing death?* Mr. Borrelli? Impossible. Mr. B wouldn't hurt a fly.

"Up and down. Up and down. The wiring was shoddy. He should have reported it. A woman died, you know ..."

The ground abandoned Jake when madness met meaning: The elevator. The wiring. Jake had known something was wrong. He had tried to tell Mr. B, but he was a ghost and Mr. Borrelli hadn't heard him. Jake could have done something to stop this. He could have saved that woman.

His mother closed the door, but Jake stuck his arm in and forced his way inside. He couldn't let her disappear.

"Think!" he yelled. "Where's Drew? I need to find Drew!"

She released the door, kicked off her shoes, and resumed humming as she walked toward the kitchen. Jake shut the door behind him. He followed her, eyeing the place as he went. Little had changed here. It was almost the same as he'd left it. The world outside had changed. St. George Station had changed. The buses had changed. The fares had changed. But here, inside apartment 710, time had stood still.

His mother made herself a pot of coffee, muttering more nonsense, oblivious to his presence. Jake felt like an intruder in his own home. He examined the space. The same cupboards. The same table and chairs, the same —

"Drew's a king," said his mother suddenly.

Jake glanced up. "What did you just say?"

"Drew's a king," she repeated, as though it was the most natural thing in the world to say.

Jake flew to her side and took a deep breath. The last thing he wanted to do was frighten her again. "A king?" he said as calmly as his shaky voice would allow.

His mother didn't look at him. She stepped around him as if he were an obstacle in her path. Opening the cupboard, she reached for a mug. "A king without a crown."

Jake's thoughts raced to solve the riddle. *A king without a crown?*

The significance of her words bulldozed him, and he fell back against the wall. He opened his mouth, but no sound came out. Jake coughed, swallowed, and coughed again. It wasn't possible. Drew was the good kid. The smart kid. Why would he do it? He didn't need them. He didn't need what little they had to offer. Drew had a bright future. Not like Jake. How could Drew do something so foolish?

Jake reached for his mother's hands and held them gently in his. "The 5 Kings? He's in the 5 King Tribe?"

His mother looked up, her eyes locking onto Jake's. And it was as if he could see the sorrow of the world puddling in them. She nodded once, then let her eyelids close. When she opened them again, she was gone.

Jake let his whole body slump against the wall. The surface was rough. He turned and ran his hand along the wall. Deep beneath the old paint, exactly where he'd etched it what seemed like only hours ago, was the eerie outline of his name.

CHAPTER TWENTY-FIVE

Jake grasped the doorknob in his sweaty palm. What would he find there? Would he find himself — ten years older — lying stretched out on his bed? Would the sight be too much to handle? Would he lose his mind just like his mother? Adrenaline coursed through his veins, setting them on fire as he let the door creak open.

A musky odour escaped the room, rushing past Jake as he peered inside. The blinds were drawn; a swampy darkness beckoned him inward. He hesitated before crossing the threshold. There was something in there. Something he shouldn't see. He could feel it clawing at him, dragging him closer.

"It's just your imagination," he muttered, and the sound of his own voice gave him strength.

He had to get in there. Jake had to locate a phone number, an address — something that might lead him to his brother. If he could find Drew, the insanity would end.

Jake flicked the light switch. Blinded by a flurry of coloured dots, his eyes slowly adjusted. He took a step inside. His bedroom hadn't changed. It was exactly the same as he'd left it. His clothes lay strewn across the floor with his school books and other junk in the exact same spot he'd left them. His bed was the same wrinkled mess. Drew's side was neat and tidy with all his stuff exactly where Jake had last seen it.

His mind raced through a labyrinth, hitting one dead end after another. Ten years had passed, and yet here, for some reason, time had stood still. It made no sense — not even for the warped and twisted realities he'd recently visited.

Something was wrong. Very wrong. Jake could feel it surrounding him, closing in on him.

Don't look!

He shut his eyes. His mind was exhausted. He didn't know which way to turn. He spun around and around, flailing his arms wildly, fending off the invisible and inexplicable foe that threatened him. Finally, empty and exhausted, he crumpled into a heap on his bed. Teetering over the edge of sanity, he let himself fall.

CHAPTER TWENTY-SIX

When Jake opened his eyes, the room was dark. He could hear his mother moving around in the kitchen, humming to herself. Sitting up, he swung his legs over the edge of the bed. How long had he been lying there? It felt like centuries. He stretched his arms and cracked his neck. His body ached. The humming grew louder, and his mother appeared in the doorway. Light leaked in from the hallway. He could make out her dark silhouette — she was carrying a tray of food. He stood up.

"Sit down, Jake," she said softly.

Her voice sounded clear. Normal. The nightmare melted away. He was home in his bedroom with his mother — his sane mother — and it was as if he had never left. It was over. It was finally over.

His mother placed the tray at the foot of the bed and pulled him down so that they were sitting side by side. She handed him a glass of cold milk. He took a sip. On the tray was a napkin, some cutlery, and a bowl of spaghetti and meatballs — his favourite. The smell of her spicy sauce filled the room.

"Mom," he whispered, putting the glass down on his nightstand. "I missed you so much."

She reached over and stroked his head. "I always knew you'd come back to me, Jake. They all said I should let go, move on, but I couldn't. I knew you'd be back, and here you are, just like I told them." She leaned in and kissed his forehead.

Back? thought Jake. The facade began to fade. He was still on that train. Still at the party.

"I kept telling everyone, *My Jake will be back*, but they didn't believe me. They said I was crazy." She tossed her head. Her hair glistened like liquid silver. "I kept everything here just the way you like it." She waved her arm around the room. "I didn't move a single thing. It's all been waiting for you. I've been waiting for you ..."

The darkness pressed in on Jake again. Questions tangled into a ball of confusion in his mind. Why hadn't she moved anything in ten years? Was it because he'd left? If he'd left, where had he gone? Where was he now?

Jake's throat was so dry that it hurt to swallow. His gaze followed his mother's hand around the room. There was something here. Something he mustn't see.

Don't look!

Jake scrunched his eyes and opened them. Drew's things were still here. But Drew hadn't left. Why had she kept all his things, too?

"Where's Drew?" he asked. "I need to find him."

The light caught the corner of her eye, and any comfort Jake had found there was blown away by what he saw.

"You're staying this time, right?" she said sharply. "You're not going anywhere ever again."

Before he knew what was happening, she reached over and picked up the knife lying on the tray. The blade caught the hall light and sent flashes of fire dancing through the shadows. Jake leaned away slowly.

"Mom," he whispered, but the word was full of fear.

"No one is ever going to leave me again," she said firmly. "No one. Especially not you."

Jake's heart pummelled his insides. "Of c-course not, Mom," he stammered. "I'm not going anywhere. Not ever again. I s-swear." He tried to stand up, but she snatched his wrist and yanked him back down.

"I love you, Jake," she said. "I love you so much."

Jake scanned the room frantically. What could he use to defend himself? All he saw were his clothes and books and all of Drew's things. Drew's karate gi was folded neatly on the dresser beside something else. Something black. What was it?

Don't look!

It was Jake's black hoodie — the one he was wearing. He reached down and touched his chest. How could it be in two places at the same time? Something was wrong. He stood up and took a step toward it.

Don't look!

His mother tightened her grip on his arm and pulled him backward. "I said you're staying right here!"

He volleyed glances from his dresser to his mother and back. In the dim light he could see the top of his hoodie. Something was wrong with it … it was torn in the centre and … something else …

"Jake!" she yelled. "Don't go! Don't leave me!"

Jake swung around just in time to see her lift the knife. He caught her wrist with his free hand and squeezed as hard as he could, digging his nails into her flesh. She screamed and dropped the knife. Jake pushed her aside and bolted from the room and out of the apartment. He could hear her sobbing wildly behind him.

"Wait!" she squealed. "Don't go, Jake! Don't leave me!"

Throwing open the metal hall door, he ducked into the stairwell and raced down flight after flight until he burst through the emergency door and into the dark night. Jake kept running until he reached the main road. Then he saw him.

CHAPTER TWENTY-SEVEN

Cole stood under a streetlamp in front of the coffee shop, lighting a cigarette. Jake barely recognized him. His hair was short and thin and his hairline had receded, making his forehead practically glow in the lamplight. He was unshaven, and he had way more wrinkles than any twenty-four-year-old Jake had ever seen. But it was his eyes that spooked Jake. Even at a distance Jake could see that the defiant flash that used to light Cole's eyes was gone. They were dull and hard — as if they'd seen a whole lot of stuff they shouldn't have.

Jake moved closer.

Cole took a long drag on his cigarette. He stared at Jake for a second, narrowed his eyes, and then blew a cloud of smoke into the air. The wind snatched the toxic fumes and dragged them off into the darkness. Cole turned and walked calmly toward the parking lot.

He has no clue who I am, thought Jake.

Cole strolled to the back of the shop with Jake only steps behind. He opened the door to a beat-up black Accord with tinted windows. Cole glanced back over his shoulder, his expression carved into a mistrusting scowl, then got into his car and yanked the door shut.

Jake stood glued to the ground. He couldn't understand why Cole hadn't recognized him. Sure, he was ten years younger — but it was still him. Why wouldn't his best friend identify him?

The engine choked to life and snapped Jake out of his trance. Cole might know where Jake could find Drew. He couldn't let him get away.

The Accord started to roll, and Jake sprang into action. He lunged toward the car and pounded on the driver's window. The brakes yelped as the vehicle lurched to a halt. All Jake could see through the tinted window was Cole's dark silhouette.

"Cole!" he shouted. "It's me. Open up."

For a moment nothing happened. Jake had raised his hand to pound on the window again when it glided open. As they stared at each other, Jake saw something else in Cole's eyes. It looked like fear.

"It's me," he said. "I need to talk to you."

Cole's eyes grew wide, then settled back into a cold, hard glare. "Get lost, kid," he growled, and the window began to rise.

Why was Cole acting this way? So Jake looked a whole heck of a lot younger, but why was he blowing him off like this? Wouldn't he want to talk to him? Wouldn't he want to find out what had happened?

The window was halfway up and the car had started to roll. Jake's pulse beat out of control. He had one shot and hoped he'd hit his mark.

"You set me up, man!" he cried. "You and Damon set me up! I heard you guys talking in the coffee shop that day!"

The car stopped. The window stopped.

"You set me up to take the fall and dragged my little brother into your mess. You owe me, man. Tell me where Drew is. Where's my brother?"

The air raced in and out of Jake's lungs. His fists were balled, preparing for confrontation, but the car just sat there, the choking engine sounding more and more like a dying animal. Then, slowly, steadily, the car rolled backward until Jake and Cole were face to face once again. Cole sized Jake up and down.

"Let's go," Cole said suddenly, motioning his head toward the passenger seat.

Jake hesitated. This wasn't going the way he'd expected. Who was this guy inviting him into his car? Jake didn't know him anymore. He was a stranger.

"Get in," Cole said. "I'll take you to see Drew — if that's what you really want."

His smoke-filled laughter sent a shiver skittering up Jake's spine.

CHAPTER TWENTY-EIGHT

The Accord rolled to a stop in front of a building a few blocks away. A group of guys hung around on the front steps. The walls behind them were covered in spray paint. There was a giant Roman numeral *V* and a capital *K*. Beneath it was an image Jake knew all too well — a crown dripping blood. There was other graffiti, too, some of which Jake understood. He knew the number four stood for the fourth letter in the alphabet. It was a warning. *D* meant *death to rivals*. There were names, too — most likely nicknames. *Shark* leaped out at Jake. He had a pretty good idea who belonged to that nickname.

Cole gave Jake a shove. "You wanted to see Drew. What are you waiting for?"

"Cole ..." Jake began, but the guy smacked him upside the head. Jake whipped around. He could feel tears of anger and embarrassment welling in his eyes. He fought them back.

"I don't know who you are, or where you get off calling me by my name," he snarled. "No one calls me that anymore, anyway. Not even my mother."

Jake gritted his teeth, swallowed his anger, and nodded. He had to see his brother. He was so close now. Drew was all that mattered.

The car door swung open. Jake's insides were a mass of jelly, but he knew better than to show any fear to these guys.

He and Cole walked up to the front of the building. As they approached, one guy stood up and blocked their path. At first Jake didn't recognize the face that appeared before him, but then he saw the tattoo emblazoned across the guy's knuckles. He had less hair and a giant scar across his face, but those steel-grey eyes ... It was Damon, all right — the Shark.

He looked at Jake, and for a second his eyes widened. They searched Cole for answers. When Cole shrugged, Damon sized Jake up and down again, then narrowed his eyes suspiciously. "Who are you?"

Why doesn't anybody know who I am? thought Jake.

"This guy wants to see Drew ..." Cole sneered. " ... Claims he's his *brother*."

Damon volleyed glances between Jake and Cole.

Jake watched a smile slither across Damon's lips. "Drew!" he called over his shoulder. "Your *brother's* here to see you!"

Jake swallowed. Something didn't feel right about the way Cole and Damon both said the word *brother*. They had been the ones who had tried to set him up all those years ago. He couldn't escape the feeling that they were setting him up again.

Drew will know me, thought Jake. *He's my brother. He'll know me.*

The group of guys parted like a curtain, and one figure emerged. He was tall and lean but looked as solid as a tank. Could it be? Was it really him? Jake resisted the urge to blink in case the vision disappeared.

With a mixture of amusement and disbelief, Drew glared at Jake. And in the instant their eyes locked, any hope Jake had that his brother might recognize him oozed into a puddle on the cold concrete steps.

Drew had changed. This wasn't the little kid he remembered. Something had happened to him. Something horrible.

Drew spat on the pavement inches from Jake's feet. "What do you want?"

Jake cleared his throat. He didn't know what to say. How would he make his brother understand?

"It's me," he said quietly. "It's *Jake*."

Drew's eyes ignited in cold flames. Jake had never seen anything like it. Who was this?

What had happened to his brother? What had changed him?

Jake heard Cole and Damon cackling as if they'd known all along Drew would react like a psycho. He opened his mouth, but before he could get another word out Drew slammed his fist into Jake's gut and the wind exploded out of his lungs.

"Jake," said Drew coldly.

Jake gasped for air. He almost snatched a mouthful of oxygen when a second fist crashed into his stomach.

"My *brother*?" Drew said.

Jake's knees buckled, and he dropped to the ground. He struggled to breathe, stealing short, shallow breaths, but it was as if there wasn't enough air left on the entire planet. His insides felt as if they'd been ripped out of him.

"My brother died," said Drew with controlled fury, "on a Sunday. Ten years ago …" He pulled back his leg and released it into Jake's side before he calmly continued. "He took the bullet that was meant for me."

Jake's mind and body were disconnected. He couldn't breathe, let alone string the meaning of his brother's words together. *Bullet? Died?* Jake battled to make the words make sense, but the meaning was all wrong. Jake wasn't dead. Not yet, anyway.

Thud! Thud! Two more kicks right to his side.

Jake's brain was a tangled mess, but one image emerged clean and clear: his hoodie. His black hoodie. Lying folded on his dresser. Torn in the centre and ... and ... covered in what might have been dried blood.

"You must be some kind of fool," Drew said, releasing his leg again and again into Jake's side. "Disrespecting my brother when tomorrow is the anniversary of his death."

It's me, thought Jake in his pain-induced haze. *I'm here. I didn't die.*

Thud!

Say something.

Thud!

And like a ghostly galleon sailing out of the fog, a memory drifted back to Jake and he found the words. "You may be a black belt ..."

Thud!

"... but I can still ... kick your butt ..."

Thud! Thud!

"... in Karate ... Chaos ..."

CHAPTER TWENTY-NINE

The beating stopped. The burning continued. Jake wasn't sure which way was up. The world spun round him as he heaved and gagged. His nose was bleeding. He could taste the metallic-sweet liquid running down his throat. Laughter echoed from all directions. He tried to look up, but his vision was fuzzy — he was seeing quadruple. What seemed like hundreds of guys crowded around him, swaying back and forth, melting in and out of one another. Jake searched the mob wildly until he found his brother.

Drew bent down, grabbed Jake by the hair, and lifted his head. Their eyes locked a second time, and this time they stared at each other for what felt like an eternity. All noises around them ceased to exist. Everything around them faded to black.

Jake watched his brother's expression transform from rage to incredulity and then to something entirely different.

"Jake?" he whispered.

Jake nodded once.

Drew's jaw trembled. He looked as if he was about to say something, but before he began a dark figure scattered the crowd and smacked Drew on the shoulder.

"What are you waiting for? Finish him off."

There was no mistaking that voice. It was Vlad.

Drew reacted quickly. He flashed Jake an expression that made Jake think of the caged tiger he'd seen at the zoo. He hauled Jake to his feet and shoved him in the direction of the street. "This trash isn't worth the effort."

Jake stumbled, nearly falling flat on his face, but caught his balance in the last moment. Even though Jake knew what Drew was trying to do, his words still cut Jake right to the bone. He turned around, and with what strength he had left, staggered back toward his brother.

The crowd went wild.

"What a loser!"

"He's coming back for more!"

Drew swung around. He took a step toward Jake and shook his head once, ever so slightly. His eyes pleaded. Then he hollered so everyone could hear, "Get outta here, kid. While you still can …"

Jake swiped the blood from his face. "No," he said firmly. "I'm not gonna lose you again."

"I thought I told you to finish him off," Vlad said. "Do it. Or *I* will."

Drew grabbed Jake by the scruff of the neck, and just before he hurled Jake toward the street, he whispered, "I'm already lost ..."

Jake felt his body being propelled forward. He landed with a *thunk* on the cold sidewalk. He couldn't believe he was responsible for Drew's involvement with these animals. Jake should never have gotten mixed up with the 5 Kings. He'd led his brother straight to them.

With all his might Jake hauled himself to his knees. As he struggled to stand, he heard the thunder of an engine rising over the jeers. It was getting louder and louder.

Then everything happened in slow motion.

The grey car appeared out of nowhere. Jake saw the crowd on the steps draw their weapons. Shots rang out. Everyone dived for cover — everyone except Drew, who had left Jake lying on the sidewalk and was walking toward the building with his back to the street. Jake screamed. He watched in horror as his brother slumped to the ground.

"No! Drew! No!"

Jake lunged forward, but his head struck something and he fell backward. He scrambled to his feet and ploughed forward with full force, but he rammed right into what felt like a brick wall. Jake searched frantically, but there was nothing there. He was trapped in an invisible cage, his eyes trained on Drew's body lying silent and still amid the chaos.

"Drew!" he screamed. He pounded his fists on the invisible barrier. "Drew!"

And then suddenly the world around him began to shrink. Smaller. Tighter. Transforming. Mutating. Closing in on him.

Jake was on the subway again, pounding on the glass window. He stared at his brother lying on the ground in a pool of his own blood, but the image was fading. It got smaller and smaller until it disappeared altogether behind the black rush of the tunnel walls.

CHAPTER THIRTY

Energy drained from Jake like water through a cracked cup. He felt numb. "It isn't real," he muttered, hugging his chest. "It isn't real ..."

"Maybe," said a familiar voice. "Then again, maybe not."

Jake looked up. Anaesthetized by grief, he barely reacted to what he saw.

A few matted clumps of hair were all Short-Shorts had left. His skin was gauze-like, his eyes cavernous. Colour had evaporated from his clothing. Jake glanced around at the other passengers. They had all deteriorated.

"You're dead," said Jake with a voice both indifferent and accepting. "I guess that means I'm dead, too."

"Maybe," repeated Short-Shorts. "Then again, maybe not ..."

A spark of hope flickered within Jake. "What I just saw — Drew — has that happened yet?"

Short-Shorts took a deep, wheezing breath. "The future is a tricky thing ..."

"Spare me the lecture. Just answer my question. Has it happened yet or not?"

Short-Shorts narrowed his eyes. "The short answer is, no, it hasn't happened. Yet …"

The spark ignited. Flames of hope danced within Jake. "Then it doesn't have to happen that way, right? It can still change?"

"Maybe. Maybe not …"

"Stop saying that!" Jake yelled. He took a step toward Short-Shorts. "If it's the future, then what if I never show up? He won't die then, will he?"

Short-Shorts shook his head. "You saw the spray of bullets. With or without you, good chance he'll catch one. Besides, look who he's hanging with. Even you're smart enough to read the writing on the wall. One way or another, it'll all end the same."

"No," said Jake. "I won't let it happen. There has to be a way. Tell me. I'll do anything."

Short-Shorts started to laugh.

"Come on!" cried Jake. "I can fix this. Let me go back. I'll go to the coffee shop and take that bullet for him. Then Drew can go home and he can …"

"Tsk-tsk," interrupted Short-Shorts. "Drew never does go home, Jake. You die in the coffee shop. Cole cuts a deal and takes Drew down with him. Drew goes to juvie — along with Cole. After that they pretty much end up in and out of jail for the next ten years. And your mom, well, we all know what happens to her …"

Jake pressed his hands to his ears and shook his head violently. "You're wrong! I can change this! I can change it all! Just give me a chance!"

A smile snaked across what was left of Short-Shorts' lips. "It's not that easy. You can't unspill milk."

Jake froze. Someone else had said that. He gave his head a shake. It didn't matter — they were wrong. He could change things. He *did* change things. For a moment he saw his father slipping through his fingers and spiralling downward.

"I already changed the past," he told Short-Shorts. "And if I can change the past, I can change the future."

The lights in the subway car began to flicker like a strobe light in a retro disco. In each second of darkness Jake saw skeletal faces closing in on him. The air was getting hotter by the second. The stench of rotting flesh hung like a cloud over him. The girl at the back of the train stopped rocking. For the first time she turned to face Jake. She held out her blanket, and Jake saw what was wrapped in it. And suddenly Jake understood exactly where he was.

He was on the train to hell.

Jake grabbed hold of Short-Shorts, and his fingers sank through the old wristbands and into the guy's skin. He drew back, gagging and coughing, struggling to force down the bile rising in his throat.

"I don't belong here," said Jake. "Not yet, anyway. You have to let me off. I have to be there to take that bullet. Drew's life depends on me."

Short-Shorts shrugged. "He's going to die, anyway, Jake. You saw it yourself. You saved him once only to hand him over to the 5 Kings where he'll die just the same. Life sucks, doesn't it?"

Demonic laughter fell like hail from the sky, sending Jake's thoughts scurrying for shelter. He scrunched his eyes. That hadn't happened yet. He wouldn't let it happen. There had to be a way. If only he could change something. Just one little thing.

As if answering his question, Short-Shorts leaned in, his breath rancid. "There *is* one thing within your power to change. You might not be able to save Drew, but you *could* save yourself. You don't have to die in that coffee shop. You don't have to take that bullet. Drew's going to die no matter what. Save yourself, Jake. Save yourself."

Jake took a step back, his head dizzy with unwanted thoughts. "No," he said, shaking his head. "No way ..."

"Choices, choices, decisions, decisions," said Short-Shorts. "Life's all about choices. Go on. Sacrifice Drew. Save yourself. Why not?"

"Shut up!" Jake screamed. "Shut up and let me off this train!"

"Oh, but Jake," asked Short-Shorts, "are you sure you don't want to hang around? It's really one *hell* of a party ..."

The zombie passengers turned to face Jake. They inched toward him, reaching for him with their bony fingers.

Is this it? he wondered. *Is this how it ends?*

But before he could finish his thought, a deafening blast shook the train as it exploded into the station. The doors behind Jake blew open. He just needed to step off and he'd be safe.

Turning to face the station, Jake put one foot safely on the platform, relief rippling through his body. He was halfway out when he felt steely talons dig into him from behind. Short-Shorts had him by the shoulder and was dragging him back onto the train.

Jake struggled to break free from the vise-like grip. Short-Shorts pulled him in close and whispered in his ear, *"Last stop."*

Then, with one foot on the train and one foot on the platform, Jake watched, paralyzed with horror, as the three-inch gap between the train and the platform doubled and tripled in size until it was the great yawning chasm he'd seen before.

The train began to roll. Jake felt his body being ripped apart. He could step backward and remain on the train — for all eternity — or he could step forward and let himself fall into the blackness below.

There was only one way to go. Jake tore himself free from Short-Shorts' grip. The last thing he heard before plummeting downward into the abyss was Short-Shorts' voice echoing through the emptiness: "Mind the gap, Jake … Mind the gap."

CHAPTER THIRTY-ONE

Free-falling, drowning in the shadows of nothingness, Jake felt his body and mind disconnecting — being wrenched in vastly opposing directions. He was losing it. Losing himself. Swirling. Twirling. Falling.

"Take my hand!"

A voice sliced through the emptiness and jolted Jake into awareness.

"Take my hand and rise!"

That voice! thought Jake. *I know it!*

As hard as he tried to focus, he couldn't seem to move his arms or his legs. Darkness smothered him, squeezing the life out of him as he spiralled downward.

"Rise up! Rise out!"

Then something snatched Jake's hand and held it tight. He felt himself being reeled in through the inky brine, upward, outward, until his head burst through the darkness and into the bright light of the subway station. A familiar face stared down at him.

"Pull yourself up! A train is coming!"

With energy born of primordial fear, Jake

swung his free hand over the edge and gripped the platform. He could hear the distant rumble of a train and felt the tracks beneath him trembling. With the homeless man's help, Jake hauled himself up and pulled his legs over the edge just in time for a subway train to screech past him. He lay on the cold concrete tiles, swallowing huge gulps of air as a crowd gathered around him.

"Did you see that?" asked one lady.

"Where'd he come from?" asked another.

One man tried to help Jake to his feet, while another shouted, "Call 911!"

No one took notice of the homeless man. As Jake stared at his rescuer, once again he saw a familiar glint in the man's eyes. Years melted from the man's face, and even through the ragged beard and matted hair and wrinkles, Jake suddenly recognized him.

"*D-dad*?" he said, his voice quaking with fear and excitement and exhaustion. "Is it really you?"

The people gathered around Jake looked puzzled. They seemed to be searching the crowd to see who he was talking to.

"He's got a concussion," said the first lady.

The homeless man gazed at Jake for the longest time. He peered down at his clothes and his hands as if his mind were emerging from the great darkness, too. He looked back at Jake and nodded slowly.

Tears of joy and regret welled in Jake's eyes. "I'm so sorry, Dad. I'm so sorry I did this to you." Jake leaned in to throw his arms around his father, then stopped short. The clock on the video screen read exactly twelve.

"Take it easy, son," said the old woman. "You've had quite a scare."

"What day is this?" he said frantically. "Can anyone tell me what day it is?"

"It's Sunday," said a man.

Twelve o'clock. Sunday. The day Jake was going to die.

CHAPTER THIRTY-TWO

Jake pulled out his phone and swore. There was no reception in the subway tunnels. "Come on," he said, grabbing his father by the ragged coat and dragging him out of the crowd toward the escalator. "There's still time. I can still save him."

Racing down the steps, Jake sped across the hall and onto an eastbound subway train, his father following close behind. As the doors sealed shut, Jake paced the floor. His father steadied himself on a post, observing him.

For the longest time neither seemed able to break the silence of lost years. Jake's mind was a disaster zone. There were so many things he had wanted desperately to say to his father. Now that he finally had the chance, he didn't know where to begin. Ten years. His father had been gone ten years. And yet somehow Jake didn't feel as if he was the stranger he should be.

"I don't know what happened …" said his father. "One day I was heading out to run a few errands, next thing I knew …"

"It's my fault," Jake interrupted, his voice trembling with emotion. "It's all my fault. You. Drew. It's all because of me ..."

His father grabbed Jake's shoulder and pulled him down into a seat. He put his arms around Jake. They were strong yet gentle arms. *Soft*, Jake thought, *like feathers. Like a pigeon.*

It was a strangely awkward moment filled with both joy and anguish. All the while Jake kept thinking, *I've got him back. I've finally got him back. And all we've got are a few hours before ...*

"Drew's in danger," Jake said. "I need to get to him."

His father nodded.

"We'll need to move fast."

Jake filled his father in as best he knew, but he purposely left out the part where he'd be taking the bullet. Jake's father listened intently, nodding, his worried expression mirroring Jake's. As soon as the doors opened at Victoria Park Station, they exited the subway and sprinted toward the buses.

When the bus rolled onto the street, Jake took out his phone and sighed with relief — he had service. He punched out his home number, but got no answer. He hung up and tried again. Where were they? Were they out looking for him? He tried again and again, and finally left a frantic message. "It's me. I'm so sorry, Mom.

I'm coming home now. If you get this message, don't let Drew out of the apartment. He's in danger — real danger. I'll be home soon."

Time was running out. As the bus jostled and bumped its way along, Jake kept thinking, *How can I make a change? A change that will save Drew both now and later ...*

"Listen, Dad," he said, choking back his emotions, "if anything happens to me, you have to convince Mom who you are. You have to make her understand. And whatever happens, you can't let Drew get involved with the 5 Kings. Promise me."

His father took a deep breath and nodded. "I made you a promise once, Jake, and I failed you. This time I won't let you down."

The bus lurched to a halt at Jake's stop. He jumped off and hurried toward the coffee shop, his father running close behind. Jake had made it in time. He swung the door open and froze. Drew wasn't there. Neither was Cole. It was twenty to one; Jake was too early.

"What's wrong?" asked his father.

Jake did an about-face, racing back toward his apartment building. "Move!" he yelled over his shoulder.

New hope coursed through his veins. *I can stop this! I can get to Drew before he leaves the apartment.*

Jake yanked out his keys and opened the lobby door. He turned toward his father, who had been following him, and held a hand to his chest.

"You can't go up. It will be too confusing. When I know Drew's safe, I'll explain everything." He let the door swing shut and bolted toward the elevators. Jake punched the buttons several times. The doors opened, and Jake stepped inside.

He hit number seven, then suddenly remembered the faulty wiring. Jake jumped off the elevator just in time. The doors closed and the car left without him. He raced toward the stairwell and charged up flight after flight until he burst through the metal door on the seventh floor.

Jake stood panting in front of his apartment. The door swung open, and his mother pounced on him. She flung her arms around Jake as if she wanted to hug him and strangle him at the same time.

"Where have you been? I've been worried sick! I swear, Jake, this time you've gone too far!" Her voice trembled with a mixture of rage and relief.

Jake thought his heart would explode as he squeezed her as tightly as he possibly could, trying to string his thoughts together. "You have no idea ... I'll never ... not ever ... I swear, this time ... You have to believe me ..."

Tears streamed down her cheeks. She pressed him into her chest. "Don't leave like that again, Jake. Don't ever ..." The rest of her sentence was swallowed by incomprehensible sobs.

Jake wanted to hold her forever, but he had to talk to Drew first. He gently pushed her away and began to walk toward the living room.

"Where's Drew? I need to talk to him. Did you get my message?"

"What message?" she asked.

Jake froze. "Drew," he gasped. "Where is he?"

"You just missed him," his mother said. "He left a few minutes ago. He said something about meeting Cole and finding you."

CHAPTER THIRTY-THREE

Jake could hear his mother calling behind him, but there was no time to explain — he hadn't a second to lose. He had sent the elevator up to the seventh floor. Drew must have taken it down. They'd just missed each other.

His mind scrambled faster than his feet. He sprinted toward the front door where his father stood waiting all alone. Drew had slipped past him. He hadn't recognized his own son. The last time his father had seen Drew he was a baby.

A young woman walked by Jake's father and entered the building.

For some reason Jake stood there watching the woman push the button and step calmly into the elevator. Jake blinked. And in that second he saw the elevator engulfed in flames and the woman screaming inside.

That's her! That's the woman. She's going to die!

Jake didn't know which way to turn. He had to get to Drew. He was already late. It was almost one. He might even be too late, but he had to try. At the same time he couldn't just let this woman die.

Then, as if emerging from a dream, he heard Short-Shorts' voice echoing around him. "Decisions ... Decisions ..."

Jake swiped at the air and sprang into action.

"Get off!" he yelled, lunging at the elevator and jamming his arm between the doors. "You have to get off! There's something wrong with the wiring!"

"Wiring?" said Mr. Borrelli, appearing behind Jake. "What are you talking about?"

"There's no time to explain. You just have to trust me, Mr. B. The elevator's broken — you need to shut it down. Now!"

The woman stepped off, looking shocked and confused. Mr. Borrelli shook his head and stepped into it himself.

"Mr. B, you have to get off!" cried Jake. He grabbed the man's arm and pulled. "Look at me. I wouldn't say this if it wasn't true. You have to trust me."

Mr. Borrelli stared at Jake. There must have been something in his eyes that convinced the old man. "Okay, Jake," he said, hitting the emergency stop button. "I'll get a sign and call for service."

Relief rippled through Jake. He had done it. He had saved that woman. And Mr. B. He had made a change. Short-Shorts was wrong. Jake did have the power to alter the future!

He exited the building and snatched his father's arm. "Did you see him? Did you see Drew pass by?"

"I ... I saw a young kid, but I didn't know it was him."

"He's gone to the coffee shop!" shouted Jake, letting go of his father and running as fast as his legs could carry him. "I can still make it! There's still time!"

CHAPTER THIRTY-FOUR

Jake tore open the door to the coffee shop. Drew sat across from Cole at a booth near the back. A brown paper bag lay on the table between them. He flew toward his brother screaming, "Drew, get away from him!"

Drew turned around, his eyes wide with shock and relief. "Jake!"

Cole stood up and put his hand on the bag. "Nice of you to decide to show," he said coldly.

"And what were you going to do if I hadn't?" said Jake, hauling Drew to his feet. He tucked his little brother in behind him and squared off against Cole. "Use Drew? He's only ten years old, Cole. What kind of sick person are you?"

Cole took his hand off the bag and pointed an accusing finger at Jake. "You stood me up at the party, and you were going to stand me up today —"

Jake reacted with lightning speed. He snatched the paper bag and held it high in the air. "Is this it, Cole? Is this what's so important to you? More important than me? More important than my kid brother?"

"You'd better give that back if you wanna stay healthy," Cole said.

Jake looked at the guy he'd called his best friend for nearly four years. He didn't know him. He was a complete stranger. Cole's eyes were glazed over. His hands were shaking. He had sunken deeper into all the 5 Kings had to offer — much deeper than Jake had realized.

"You need some serious help, man," said Jake. "I'm taking this to the cops."

Rage spread like wildfire across Cole's cheeks. Then it happened — so fast and so slow at the same time. The world around Jake evaporated.

Cole reached into the back of his pants, pulled out a gun, and pointed it at Jake. "Gimme the bag."

Chaos erupted. Gasps and screams sliced through the white noise. Chairs scraped across the cheap floor as the other customers dived for cover. Drew sobbed behind Jake, pressing into the small of his brother's back.

Jake summoned whatever courage he had left. "No," he said firmly. He started to back up, inch by inch, keeping Drew safely tucked behind him. "Put it down, Cole. We can all walk away from this."

Cole's eyes flashed white-hot. "It's too late. I'm in too deep. I owe Vlad more money than

I'll ever make in my whole life. He'll cut me loose if I do this favour for him. If I screw up, I'm fish food. I'd rather take my chances in juvie."

In the distance Jake could hear sirens approaching, but the noise was faint — they were too far away.

"You're fooling yourself," said Jake, trying to buy some time. "They'll never cut you loose, Cole. Not ever."

"Give me the freakin' bag!" screamed Cole. "Or I'll … I'll …"

"What? You'll shoot me?" Jake kept backing up, slowly, carefully, as if he were walking on daggers. He was partway to the door.

The gun quaked in Cole's grasp. Sweat streamed down his cheeks in tiny rivulets.

"Come on, Cole," Jake said. "You're not like them. You're no killer. You won't pull that trigger."

Cole's hands were shaking so hard that Jake was sure the gun would slip from his hands.

"Come on, man," repeated Jake.

Cole stared at Jake for the longest time, the ice in his eyes beginning to melt. Then, slowly, deliberately, he lowered the weapon.

Relief loosened the noose around Jake's neck. He could breathe again. "I knew you wouldn't do it," he whispered.

It was the wrong thing to say.

Cole's eyes flashed with a hatred and rage so fierce in that instant that he looked more animal than human. In the same moment Drew stepped out from behind Jake.

"Get back!" Jake screamed, reaching for his brother.

Cole raised the gun and aimed. Jake watched in paralyzed horror as Cole's fingers squeezed the trigger. Jake dived in front of his brother and shut his eyes. He heard the shot ring out and waited for the impact ...

CHAPTER THIRTY-FIVE

The pain didn't come. Opening his eyes, Jake felt his chest. There was no hole there. No blood. He could hear his brother sobbing nearby. They were both alive.

Jake glanced down. Lying motionless on the floor in a sea of blood between him and Cole was his father. Cole was wide-eyed, still holding the gun, when the police stormed into the coffee shop. He dropped it, and it landed on the floor next to Jake's father. The police converged on Cole in a flash, knocking him to the ground and pinning him.

Jake scrambled to his father's side, taking his hand.

"No, Dad," he whispered. "I can't lose you again." His father squeezed his hand once and then it went limp. "Help!" Jake cried. "Help, someone! Get an ambulance!"

The last words faded back into Jake's throat.

"Who are you talking to?" Drew asked, approaching Jake from behind.

Jake looked up at the chaos around him. No one was taking any notice of his father.

"I shot him!" Cole yelled. "I shot him straight in the heart!"

The police cuffed Cole and were dragging him out of the coffee shop.

"You saw me!" he shouted to everyone around him. "You saw me shoot him! Where's the bullet? Where did the bullet go?"

Jake searched the sea of faces. They were all staring at Jake. Then Jake glanced down at his father. Like smoke in the wind, his body started to fade until it disappeared altogether.

Cole was still screaming when the door to the coffee shop closed. He was kicking and struggling. For a split second he managed to gaze back at Jake. Their eyes locked for a second, and in that instant the coffee shop melted away and Jake was standing on the train one last time. The passengers, now nothing more than wraithlike creatures, hovered in front of Jake. They split like a curtain and drifted apart. For the first time Jake got a clear look at the lone figure sitting at the back of the subway. The figure turned to face Jake.

It was Cole. He had been riding that train all along.

Something grabbed Jake, dragging him out of his trance. He was back in the coffee shop again. Drew was hugging him and crying.

They were safe — both of them. Jake had

made the change. He'd made it when he first stepped onto that subway.

As the two brothers stepped out of the coffee shop and into the bright light of day, Jake's phone vibrated. He pulled it out of his pocket and read the text: *Choices, choices. Decisions, decisions. Party's waiting, Jake. Party's waiting …*

Jake put an arm around his brother, flipped his phone shut, and tossed it into the trash.

Accomplice
by Valerie Sherrard
978-1-55488-764-4
$9.99

Lexie Malton is an average Vancouver teen with fairly typical issues. Her stepmother is far from her favourite person, she has a sister with special needs, and life outside the home is the usual mix of school, friends, and social events. But Lexie has a secret. Her ex-boyfriend, Devlin Mather, is now a heroin addict living on the street, and only Lexie knows that she's the one who put him there. Guilt makes her give in to Devlin's demands for money time and time again, even though she knows how dangerous his drug use is. Lexie finally gathers the strength to stop enabling Devlin. But when he seeks treatment for his addiction, Lexie finds herself drawn back to him, never guessing what a dark and deadly path she has just chosen.

Lure
by Deborah Kerbel
978-1-55488-754-5
$12.99

Absolutely nothing is going right for Max Green. His parents have just uprooted their family from Vancouver to the bleak suburbs of Toronto, he has no friends, and everybody at his new high school is ignoring him. To make matters worse, he's in love with an older girl who's completely out of his league. When Max discovers a local library rumoured to be haunted by ghosts, he's immediately drawn to it. With the help of some cryptic messages, he begins to piece together the identity of the teenage ghost and the mysterious chain of events that have connected its spirit to the building for more than a century.

Available at your favourite bookseller.

DUNDURN PRESS
www.dundurn.com

What did you think of this book?
Visit **www.dundurn.com** for reviews, videos, updates, and more!